LUCK

The Complete

BLACK MASK

Cases of Oscar Sail

LESTER DENT

---

introduction by Will Murray

illustrations by Arthur Rodman Bowker

cover by John Drew

BLACK MASK

2021

Associate Editor: Ray Riethmeier

Table of Contents

Introduction

LESTER DENT WAS a remarkable writer. His Doc Savage adventure novels are still read in the 21st century and celebrated for their influence on seminal superheroes Superman, Batman, Challengers of the Unknown, The Fantastic Four, as well as enduring media properties such as *The Man from U.N.C.L.E.*, *Star Trek*, *Buckaroo Banzai*, and others.

He sold only two stories to *Black Mask* magazine, but they remain among the most anthologized tales ever printed in that legendary periodical.

Lester Dent had two favorite pulp magazines which he read faithfully: *Argosy* and *Black Mask*. He was particularly fond of Dashiell Hammett, and emulated his objective style of writing, which he brought to his earliest fiction, including his long-running Doc Savage adventure novels.

At the end of December, 1930, Dent relocated to New York City from Tulsa, Oklahoma, to become a staff writer for Dell Magazines. Lester later recalled:

> When I entered the office of Richard E. Martinsen, the Dell official who had sent me the telegram, he tossed a copy of Dashiell Hammett's latest book at me and said, "This is the sort of thing we want you to do. For what impresses us about your writing is the fast movement, the brittle violence of emotion and action."

Dent would have been astounded to learn that Hammett

would one day become a reader of *Doc Savage Magazine.* According to his daughter, Hammett read it faithfully.

At the end of 1932, Lester Dent began writing Doc Savage. He was three years into his Doc Savage career when he began itching to break out from under the restrictions of writing under the house name of Kenneth Robeson. So he took a shot at cracking the pages of *Argosy* and *Black Mask* magazines under his own name.

This was an important step in his writing career, for Dent was beginning to feel that he should start aiming for the slick magazines. But before he could make that jump, he would have to reestablish his own name with some of the more prestigious pulps.

By 1936, Carroll John Daly and Dashiell Hammett had moved on, and the stars of *Black Mask* were Raymond Chandler, Frederick L. Nebel, Theodore A. Tinsley, George Harmon Coxe, Erle Stanley Gardner, and others. Now, with Shaw approaching his tenth anniversary as *Black Mask* editor, Lester Dent aimed to join that illustrious company.

Circa 1935, Lester toyed with submitting something to *Black Mask.* A surviving notebook mentions a story idea called "Hard Country," which he intended to submit to editor Joseph T. "Cap" Shaw. It was likely going to be set in either Oklahoma or Missouri, where Dent spent his formative years. But Dent never wrote that story. A better idea hit him.

During this period, Lester wintered on his schooner, *Albatross,* a Chesapeake "bugeye" that he moored at Miami's City Yacht Basin when he wasn't cruising the Florida keys.

Lester wasn't in Miami when the historic Great Labor Day Hurricane of 1935 hit. It was the largest and most destructive

hurricane ever to hit Florida up to that time, a Category 5 with gusts of nearly 200 miles per hour. Tearing through the Florida Keys, it demolished a work camp of World War I veterans, who were constructing a highway, killing some 250 of them before an evacuation train could arrive. In all, more than 400

Floridians perished in the monster storm. It was a tremendous scandal at the time.

Dent's boat survived, but was damaged.

A second storm, the Miami Hurricane of 1935, struck Miami Beach on November 4, causing flooding, property damage, and significant erosion of the Miami Beach Causeway, but relatively few deaths, thanks to advance warnings.

By New Year's Day 1936, Dent was back in Miami, overseeing repairs to the *Albatross*. Sailing for the Keys, he inspected the damage done and searched Matecumbe for veteran bodies, which were still being discovered. He saw firsthand railroad tracks that had been twisted into weird shapes by the punishing winds. A boat had been driven a quarter mile inland. The sight of all this destruction had an impact on Lester's creative soul.

Lester also had his brush with bad blows. As he later wrote:

I incidentally expended nearly two years hunting for pirate treasure in the Caribbean, and actually found the galleon we were hunting. In it was supposed to be a gold table of nearly three tons weight—just a trifling sum of three or four million dollars. We blew the hell out of that galleon, taking it apart a splinter at a time, all but the sterncastle, then a little pup of a hurricane piled us on the reef one night. When I got the schooner off, I got out of there and never went back. The table may be there. I'm not as curious about it as I was.

According to the ship's log, Dent spent three consecutive days at the end of March writing "Sail," his first submission to *Black Mask*.

Years later, Lester described his first meeting with Shaw, at the Madison Avenue offices of *Black Mask:*

In my own case, I'd written a lot of published pulp, many millions of words of it, before I assembled enough guts to decide I might, just might, be able to do something near Cap's standard. So I telephoned him. Could I have a talk with him. I could. I went to the *Black Mask* office, expecting to get the customary puzzling generalities about what he wanted.

My first shock: Here was a cultured man editing a pulp. Second, here was an editor who thought his writers were truly great. I never did feel fully at ease that afternoon—three or four hours as I recall—because culture makes me itch, and an editor who didn't pretend his writers were crud-factories was unbelievable.

But here was a man who could breathe that pride of his into a writer. Cap didn't think I was a pulp hack. Joe felt I was a writer in step with the future. He thought that of all his writers. He had a way, with this device or some other device, of breathing power into his writers. I am sure all of Cap's writers—Hammett, Chandler, Gardner, the rest, probably felt this.

That day Shaw showed me a bit from a letter from Chandler, a piece so delicate and sensitive and perceptive that it forever moulded my view of Chandler, whom I have never met. The bit concerned some value Chandler was seeking, a thing that Shaw might congeal. Showing me the note from Chandler did exactly what Shaw probably wanted it to do—it sold me on the idea that I was not to sit down and do a hack hardboiled piece of pulp for Black Mask. I was to believe and feel I was doing a great piece.

Although the *Abatross* log records Lester working on "Sail" between March 30 and April 1st, he doesn't seem to have submitted the manuscript right away. He may have revised it after his first meeting with Shaw. In any case, Shaw's letter of rejection was dated July 19:

Dear Lester Dent:

We're simple folk; really—we've kidded ourselves so long in trying to gauge average intelligence receptivity that for all practical purposes we're it.

Style—we were unwary enough to state that we weren't concerned with style, method or technique so long as entertainment should be provided. Perhaps we are still right about that, since understanding must introduce entertainment and stand by throughout.

You've done things with this darned good story "Sail"—particularly with the first half. You've given a series of pictures that are designed to provide movement, plot and its development. Some of these pictures are gorgeous in their plentitude of descriptive material of a rare authenticity and almost as rare recognizability. Mr. Average Reader would have to go through the dictionary a

score of times to a page. In the first place, he hasn't the dictionary, and in the second, if he had, it is extremely doubtful if he would bestir himself to do so even once. He doesn't appreciate the value of such pearls, and he'd say "Nuts" or "Rats"—or some equally absurd and irrefutable New Deal argument.

So what?

Your method of presenting the story by the disjointed picture system, plus the remarkably full amplification of each, ties up Mr. Average Reader in a confused maelstrom of noddle aches more severe than Sail's cramps. You are all together too nimble for him in their swift sequences and in the still remaining too abrupt scene and angle changes.

There are approximately seventeen pages of this—and it's a darned good story. And would it lose any of its effectiveness if these seventeen pages were told in the straight-running, non-switching, simple narrative language of Mr. Average Reader?

Confidentially—many of those pictures fascinate me; but that was when I relapsed from my role. And in it once more, I am convinced that this method doesn't beget clarity and constant understandability, and without these we are gutted and sunk.

Man, can you write.

Incidentally, this is not the *Black Mask* method. It is not

Hammett's. Curiously, it chances to be exactly Jim Moynahan's conception of Hammett's style or method. Jim is so far wrong that his machinery creaks and moans. Yours does not; you have oiled it so darn well. But it is there—in places in the first seventeen odd pages, and it confuses and obfuscates, when the narrative should ring as clear as the winding of the silver horn on a winter morning.

How's your patience?

I'd tackle the do-over on this part myself—for sake of the work you've given it—but I couldn't do it justice. I'm not that much of a sailorman, and there are some pearls that must be saved.

In a postscript, Shaw added:

How about thinking of the angle of having the characters informing the reader in these pages—whereas now the author does it for the most part?

Lester seems to have gone overboard in his desire to achieve a different effect. His Doc Savage habit of using Thesaurus words played him false as well.

It's not clear what draft of "Sail" this was. The reference to Dent's Thesaurus vocabulary doesn't seem to fit any surviving draft of the manuscript.

Normally, Lester would junk a reject like "Sail" and start a substitute yarn. But this was *Black Mask*. Applying himself, Lester rewrote and revised "Sail," substantially retaining the storyline but re-imagining Oscar Sail as a very different personality. Shaw bought the revised story. It was a major sale, as significant as his first. It meant Lester had arrived as a pulp writer. He was on his way to better paper.

"Sail" is set around the familiar City Yacht Basin in Miami. It's a treasure hunt in the guise of a detective yarn. Dent's detective is Oscar Sail, absurdly tall, laconic, and habitually dressed in black. He operates a one-man Marine Investigations agency out of his jet-black schooner, a Chesapeake Bay bugeye called *Sail*—evidently after himself. (The *Albatross* was white and lacked the five-log hull described in the story.)

The Miami Sail operates in is still shrugging off the effects of the November hurricane.

Shaw ballyhooed the story thusly:

> And here's another novitiate to Black Mask, although not in the writing game—LESTER DENT; and he heralds his entry with a fresh-new, hard-fast story "SAIL," which is calculated to establishing well up among the favorites with promise of great things to come.

Lester wasted no time in moving on to a second Oscar Sail story. He started a yarn called "Angelfish," about a radio singer named Sterling Drew, but after three pages stopped cold. He may have noticed he had slipped into a quasi-Kenneth Robeson voice.

Starting over, Lester came up with the memorable first line "The fish shook its tail as the knife cut off its head." "Angelfish" has been correctly termed a tour de force. Here, a tropical storm plays a major role.

"Angelfish" sold in late August after the expected rewrite suggestions. Shaw gave it the cover of the December issue. Lester was in solid at *Black Mask*. Again, Shaw made a big deal of Dent's effort:

Lester Dent, who gave us that refreshingly "different" story, "SAIL" in October, has come straight forward with another story of Sail, an even more refreshing and startling tale of human strife while mild zephyrs are tying knots in steel rails and setting shipping in the mangroves a half mile from the coast. We'd like to put four stars against "ANGELFISH," but see for yourself how you like it.

"Sail" had no sooner seen print in the October issue than another of the many Dent career calamities struck like a searing thunderbolt.

Like so many mid-Depression era pulp magazines, *Black Mask* was losing readers. On September 1, the magazine moved from 578 Madison Avenue to number 515. "Angelfish" was one of the last stories Shaw purchased at the old stand. Presumably, the move was an austerity measure. The owners next attempted to cut Shaw's healthy salary. Shaw balked, quitting instead. After a solid decade helming *Black Mask,* Joe Shaw was out pounding the pavement like lesser mortals.

This came as a shock to the denizens of the Pulp Jungle. Dent received the news in a letter. He took it hard. But in the few short months he had worked with Cap Shaw, he developed an incredible loyalty. Lester began opening doors all over New York for Shaw.

Henry W. Ralston and John L. Nanovic called him up to Street & Smith to discuss launching a new high-quality detective pulp. Nothing came of the meeting. Another meeting to discuss launching a *Junior Reader's Digest* also came to naught.

Lester meanwhile returned to Missouri to campaign for the reelection of Franklin Roosevelt and other Democrats.

Shaw wrote him again on October 8:

Dear Lester Dent:

Each day since you left I've been wanting to write you, and then I've put it off in the hope of some definite development. I guess you know how these things go. I'll give you at least some idea of my mental occupation.

Now, what are you doing? Have you written a third Sail story? Will you send it directly to me when it's finished? Oh, yes; Chandler and Stinson are sending me their work to look over; Ballard and Babcock are going to. So, you see, I'd be only too glad if you would do so also. I've an idea the new one will be too good for *B.M.* as it is becoming. Confidentially, I find some of the fellows are sending in their rejects, and getting away with it. What happens to the magazine, I shouldn't worry about. What effect it will have on the writers is another matter, and a very serious one, as I see it; that is, if they have the ambition to go up.

This is a long letter, and between speeches, you may get an opportunity to read parts of it. But I owe it to you. And I want very much to hear from you. And I want that next Sail story, and anything else up the line you are doing. And I'll damned well find a market for them. Did I tell you what Chandler had to say about Sail? I did not, and I'll spare your blushes now. He said it couldn't be done again, and I told him to read Angelfish.

So, lemme hear from.

On October 19, Lester heard from the new editor, Fanny Ellsworth, who had previously edited the wildly successful *Ranch Romances:*

Dear Mr. Dent:

How are the electioneering activities progressing, and what are the chances of your doing *Black Mask* another story?

You'll be glad to know that I've heard only the most favorable comment on your Sail story, and so I think the wise thing to do would be to continue them.

Incidentally, in Angelfish, which appears in the December issue, you'll notice that we did a bit of simplifying of the geological angle. We got our data for the changes from a geologist for the Sinclair Oil people, because we didn't want to spoil the feeling of authenticity in the story.

Perhaps after you've done a few more stories about Sail, you'll get an idea for another character; but we can talk that over when you're back in town.

I remember with interest your idea of letting Sail do his stuff in some foreign ports. Down in the Caribbean, perhaps. How about something along those lines for the next one?

Back in La Plata, Missouri, Dent replied with a vague maybe. In fact, he did start a third Sail opus, set in warmer waters. It opened with another memorable line: "She was a fair, lean-limbed woman who swam through the dark water in her naked skin."

Unfortunately, Dent broke off after two pages, apparently abandoning the tale.

One page exists of what might be yet another Sail attempt. This one was called "Deep."

Fanny Ellsworth kept at Lester over the next three months, trying to pry loose a new Sail story, but Lester couldn't be bothered. *Black Mask* for him was a dead issue. It was a tragedy.

For a few brief weeks, Lester was Joe Shaw's newest discovery, a successor to Hammett and sharing the same pages with Raymond Chandler. But he had only a month to enjoy the spotlight before Shaw was off the magazine.

He next tried to crack *Detective Fiction Weekly* with another nautical Miami detective. Marine Investigator Cyrus Peace was the protagonist of "Windjam," which *DFW* rejected at the end of 1936 and which Dent later rewrote as a Click Rush story for *Crime Busters*.

As much a triumph as appearing in *Black Mask* was, the experience had been bittersweet, as Lester's friend and fellow writer Frank Gruber later recalled:

> Along about 1936 Lester Dent began to tire of Doc Savage. He thought the stories were too juvenile and he thought that he should be trying to write more adult fiction. He wrote two stories for *Black Mask* but he told me that he had been forced to rewrite both stories so many times that he did not himself like the final product. Also, the time and effort consumed by the long rewriting were not compensated by the modest payment of *Black Mask*. As far as I know those were the only stories that Dent sold to a 'better' pulp and Lester was greatly dissatisfied.

Yet in the decades that followed, the three most anthologized *Black Mask* contributors would be Hammett, Chandler—and on the strength of only two stories, Lester Dent.

Joe Shaw ended up with the Wilson, Powell and Hayward Literary Agency. He immediately started signing up several *Black Mask* writers. Lester joined that group. By this time, he had decided upon breaking into the slick magazines in earnest.

Under Shaw's careful tutelage, Dent began turning out count-
less slick stories, many with a Florida boating background.

Alas, none of them sold. Writer Frank Gruber remembered
Dent's unhappiness with the state of his career at that time:

> Along about 1938 and 1939, Lester came out to our place in
> Scarsdale frequently and discussed his writing efforts at length. He
> had decided to try the slicks and it was very discouraging. He was
> getting reject after reject and complained bitterly that the years of
> writing Doc Savage and ruined him for "better" writing. He had
> taken on an agent, a former famous pulp editor, who is having him

rewrite and rewrite every slick effort until all the life and spontaneity was gone from his work. No matter how much he rewrote the stories, they still did not sell. Eventually Lester sold one story to *Collier's,* but he wrote at least thirty stories before he made his single sale and it was only after he ditched the rewriting agent.

One story may have been the abortive attempt at a third Sail novelette, which Dent entitled "Cay." This was turned into a slick story, "Jungle Impulse," with the hero changed from Oscar Sail to Tom Sail. It's a typical slick formula story with the violence underplayed and the romance element pumped up. A thread running through all of these stories—the American oil industry—was no accident. Dent had worked in the Oklahoma oil fields during his pre-writing days.

Continuing in that vein, Dent turned out a similar story, "Two Kukulcans," with a new nautical character, Seaworthy Smith. It's enough in the vein of a Dent adventurer who lives on a boat that we thought we should include it. For all we know, originally this is going to be another Oscar Sail story.

During this difficult time, Lester dropped Joe Shaw as his agent and went with Willis Kingsley Wing. His luck did not improve until near the end of the 1940s.

One related project Dent worked on was a 1940 novel, *Mystery About a Fainting Dog*. The detective hero was named Homer Sail. When not detecting, Sail liked to go on round-the-world sailing trips in his own boat. Unfortunately for him, he was shipwrecked and lost his boat, and was forced back to sleuthing. When this story failed to sell, Lester rewrote it with a different protagonist, removing the sailing background.

Obviously, Lester liked the last name Sail for nautical heroes. Early in his Doc Savage career, he submitted a short story for the back of the magazine under the pseudonym of Heck Sailing. The tale ran under his own name, inasmuch as Street & Smith insisted on using a house name on the Doc novels.

Dent never looked back or attempted to sell to *Black Mask* again. But a decade after those stories had first appeared, they were so well-remembered they became sought-after for anthologies.

When Joe Shaw began picking his story selection for *The Hard-Boiled Omnibus* in 1945, he chose "Sail" for inclusion with greats like Hammett and Chandler. In his introduction, Shaw wrote of Dent:

> Lester has preferred to expend his talents on … the rough paper field. However, we believe there are elements and a treatment in the story presented here that point the way to more ambitious accomplishments, which we have an idea will be substantiated when Lester turns seriously to novels.

At about the same time, *Ellery Queen's Mystery Magazine* sought rights to that story. But they were tied up, so *EQMM* settled for "Angelfish," retitling it "Tropical Disturbance." A few years later they got around to reprinting "Sail," under the title "X Marks the Spot."

Lester was by this time writing crime novels for the Crime Club, and he revived Oscar Sail indirectly in his 1948 novel, *Lady Afraid*, featuring a protagonist, a hard-bitten boat designer who lives on a bugeye schooner, and is known only as Captain Most. Why Dent didn't call him Oscar Sail is unclear. But the characters have striking similarities, although they are distinctly different personalities.

Dent finally cracked the slick market during the last decade of this life, but not with detective characters. Westerns were big, and Lester had been raised on various ranches. By that time, Shaw no longer represented him.

Near the end of his life, Dent received a letter from Philip Durham of the University of California, who was working on a research project with colleague E.R. Hagemann on the heyday of *Black Mask* magazine.

Lester wrote back a long and informative letter about those days, dated October 27, 1958:

Dear Durham:

I don't foam easily, I'm pretty sure. But this chip of recognition you toss toward Cap Shaw and his *Black Mask* stirs my juices quite a bit.

Shaw was the finest coachwhip I ever met in an editor's chair. In my thirty-five years of free lancing fiction, no one stands out so. Hence I presume when you speak of *Black Mask* you speak of Joe Shaw.

Black Mask in Cap Shaw's hands was akin to a writer's shrine. I don't mean today, but in the Twenties and Thirties when Shaw presided. That was the brief wonderful time when American literature was endowed with the most effective training ground in all history—the pulp magazine. The writers whom Shaw published in *Black Mask* were sort of automatically endowed with a hair shirt that they wore with pride and some dubiousness, because where writers got together you were pointed out as a *Black Mask* man, not a *Post* writer, a *Collier's* writer, a *Doc Savage* writer or an *Argosy* writer, but as a *Black Mask* writer.

So Cap Shaw had recognition in his day.

His writers regarded Captain Shaw with—if any writers ever truly gave an editor such—reverence. At least I never heard a *Black Mask* writer be casual about Shaw.

My tenure with Cap Shaw was short. I sold him, I think, only three pieces. Then he gave up the helmsmanship of *Black Mask* over a policy dispute, which, I am convinced, is what kept me from becoming a fine writer. Had I been exposed to the man's cunning hand for another year or two, I could not have missed. Cap did try to work with me and guide me after he left *Black Mask,* and became an agent. But in those days I was ficety and greedy, and also Joe no longer had the money-apple to dangle in front of me—a sale to

Black Mask. Instead I wrote reams of salable crap which became my pattern, and gradually there slipped away that bit of power with words that Shaw had started awakening in me.

How did Shaw find and develop so many great writers? I wish I knew.

Joe used his coach whip in strange gentle ways. He would start discussing his writers, their skill, and before you knew it you would find some Hammett or Chandler in your hands along with a blue pencil and Cap would be asking, "Would you cut that somewhere. Just cut a few words." The idea, of course, was that there was no wordage fat. You could not cut. Every word had to be there.

You will hear it said Joseph Shaw told his writers what to write and how, demanded they do *"Black Mask"* style. This was not true. He demanded nothing of the sort. He did demand that every word mean something—he must be able to hardly touch your piece with a blue pencil. And he didn't rewrite himself—if there was one paragraph off, you got it back to re-do. That may be the secret of realism Shaw writers acquired. Anyway, when you did something lean and powerful, no excess wordage anywhere, then you had *"Black Mask* style."

Cap had above all the power to impress you incredibly with the importance of the things he considered made a good story. This may have been partly the force of his dignity, his culture. As I wrote in the beginning, I have never met another like him. Possibly as a measure of my respect for him, I never troubled to submit another piece to the *Black Mask* market after he left, a thing I certainly did not discuss with him or with anyone but myself.

I do hope you fellows grasp the idea that *Black Mask* was Joseph T. Shaw. He created its power.

My best to you,

Lester Dent

In his introduction to *The Hard-Boiled Omnibus*, Cap Shaw wrote at length about what has become branded as the hard-boiled school of writing. Therein, he gave Lester Dent the ultimate recognition for his contributions, modest as they were:

> The contributors of this brittle style were, notably, Hammett, Raymond Chandler, Raoul Whitfield, George Harmon Coxe, Roger Torrey, Forrest Rosaire, Paul Cain, Lester Dent, among others.

But were they so modest? Lester Dent's influence on popular culture has been widely acknowledged. While it's impossible to document at this late date, who is to say that Oscar Sail did not live on in the exploits of later boat-dwelling Florida detectives such as *Doc Savage* contributor John D. MacDonald's Travis McGee, Warner Bros.' *Surfside 6*, and *Miami Vice's* Sonny Crockett?

For the first time, every Oscar Sail exploit and associated story are gathered together in one volume, including the earliest original version of "Sail," which has appeared only once before under the title, "Luck." This is a landmark collection, and long overdue.

—Will Murray

Sail

A lot of costly baubles get lost, and a whole lot of men get hurt trying to find them

THE FISH SHOOK its tail as the knife cut off its head. Red ran out of the two parts and the fluid spread enough to cover the wet red marks where two human hands had failed to hold to the dock edge.

Oscar Sail wet the palm of his own left hand in the puddle.

The small policeman kept coming out on the dock, tramping in the rear edge of glare from his flashlight.

Sail split the fish belly, shook it over the edge of the yacht dock and there were some splashes below in the water. The stuff from the fish made the red stain in the water a little larger.

When the small policeman reached Sail, he stopped and gave his cap a cock. He looked down at Sail's feet and up at Sail's head.

The cop said, "Damned if you ain't a long drink of water."

Sail said nothing.

The cop asked, "That you give that yell a minute ago?"

Sail showed plenty of teeth so that his grin would be seen in the moonlight. He picked up the fishhook and held it close to his red-wetted left palm.

"Little accident," he said.

When the cop put light on the hand, Sail tightened the thumb down and made a wrinkle in the palm. Red was squeezed out of the wrinkle and two or three drops fell on the dock. It was enough like seepage from a cut the fishhook might have torn that Sail went on breathing.

"Hook, eh?" the cop said vaguely.

He put the toe of his right shoe into the fish head's open mouthful of snake-fang teeth.

"Barracuda," he added, not sounding as if that was on his mind. "They don't eat 'em in Miami. Not when you catch the damn things in the harbor, anyhow."

Sail's laugh did not go off so well and he turned it into a throat clearing.

He said, "People get hot ideas."

The policeman did not say anything and began spearing around with his flashlight beam. He poked it over the edge of the dock at one of the fish organs floating on the stained water. He held it there for what seemed a year.

After he finally began pointing the beam at other places, the light located the bugeye. The bugeye was tied at the end of the dock with springlines. Sloping masts were shiny and black and black canvas covers were on the sails. The hull looked black, neat, new.

The cop dabbed his light up and down each of the two bugeye masts and asked, "Yours?"

Sail said, "Yep."

"What you call that kind of a boat?"

Sail began talking heartily about the boat.

He said, "Chesapeake Bay five-log bugeye. She is thirty-four feet long at the waterline and forty-five overall. Her bottom is made out of five logs drifted together with Swedish iron rods. She has twelve foot beam and only draws a little over two feet of water with the centerboard up. A bugeye has sloping masts. You tell 'em by that, and the clipper bow they always put on them. They're made—"

"Yeah," the cop said. "Uh-huh."

He splashed light on Sail.

Sail would have been all right if he had been a foot or two shorter. His face would never wear a serious look successfully. Too much mouth. Sun and salt water was on its way to ruining his hair. Some of the black had been scrubbed out of his black polo shirt and black dungarees. Bare feet had long toes.

Weather had gotten to all of the man a lot.

The policeman switched off his light.

"That was a hell of a funny yell," he said. "And damned if you aren't the tallest thing I ever saw."

He stamped his feet as he walked away.

SAIL SHUT AND opened his eyes slowly and by the time he got rid of the effects of the flashlight, the officer was out of sight on shore.

Sail held both hands out about a foot from his eyes. There was enough moonlight for him to see them. A slight breeze made coolness against one side of his face. Loud music came from the Take-a-Sail-in-the-Moonlight-for-a-Dollar-a-Couple boat at the far end of the City Yacht Basin, but a barker spoiled the effect of the music. Two slot machines chugged alongside the lunch stand at Pier Six.

After he had watched his hands tremble for a while, Sail picked up hook, line, fish, knife, and got aboard the bugeye.

Sail, name of the bugeye, was in white letters on the black life preservers tied to the main stays.

Sail grasped a line, took half hitches off a cleat, and pulled a live-box made of laths partly out of the water. Some crawfish, crabs and two more live barracuda were in the live-box. He cut the line close to the live-box and let the weighted box sink.

The tiny cabin of the bugeye had headroom below for a man of ordinary height. Sail had to stoop. The usual gear was neatly, in places cleverly, stowed in the cabin.

Sail popped the fish into a kettle in the galley, hurrying.

With the point of the fishhook, he gouged a small place in his left palm, making faces over the job.

He straightened out the stuff in the tackle locker enough to get rid of signs that a hook and line had been grabbed out in haste.

After he had washed and held the mouth of a mercurochrome bottle against the gouge, he looked out of the hatch.

The young policeman was back where the fish had bled and was using his flashlight. He squatted and picked up the fish head. He squeezed it and got fresh blood out of it. After a while, he stood up and approached the dock end. When his flashlight brightened the bugeye's dark sloping masts and black sail covers, Sail was at the galley, making enough noise cutting up the fish to let the cop know where he was and what he was doing.

Sail let four or five minutes pass before he put his head out of the hatch and looked. Perspiration had made the back of his polo shirt moist by then.

The cop had gone somewhere else.

Sail was still looking and listening for the policeman when he heard a man yell and a woman curse.

The woman said, "Dam' stinker!" and more that was worse.

The man's yell was just a yell.

The sounds came out of Bayfront Park, which lay between the yacht basin and Biscayne Boulevard.

Sail got out on deck and stretched his neck around. He saw a man run among the palms in the park. The man was alone.

Then the small policeman and his flashlight appeared among the palms. During the next five minutes, the policeman and his flashlight were not motionless long enough for him to have found anything.

Sail dropped into the bugeye cabin and stripped naked,

working fast. His body looked better without clothes. The hair on it was golden and long, but not thick. He put on black jersey swim trunks.

Standing in the companion and looking around, his right hand absently scratched his chest. No one was in sight.

He got over the side without being conspicuous.

The water had odor and its normal quota of floating things. The tide was high slack, almost, but still coming in a little. Sail swam under the dock.

The dock had been built strongly because of the hurricanes. There was a net of cross timbers underneath, and anything falling off the south side of the dock would be carried against them by the tide.

Sail counted pilings until he knew he was under the place on the dock where he had used the fish. He began diving and groping around underwater. He was quiet about that.

He found what he was seeking on the sixth or seventh dive. He kept in the dark places as he swam away with it.

One of the little islands in the harbor seemed to be the only place that offered privacy. He made for it.

THE ISLAND—AN ARTIFICIAL half acre put there when they dredged the City Yacht Basin—was a heap of dark silence when Sail swam tiredly to it. Pine trees on the island had been bent by the hurricanes, some uprooted. The weeds did not seem to have been affected.

Sail tried not to splash coming out of the shallows onto the sand beach. He towed the Greek under water as long as possible.

Two stubborn crabs and some seaweed hung to the Greek

when Sail carried him into the pines and weeds. The knife sticking in the Greek, and what it had done, did not help. Weeds mashed under the body when Sail laid it down.

Pulpy skins in the Greek's billfold were probably greenbacks, and stiffer, smaller rectangles, business cards. Silver coins, a pocket knife, two clips for an automatic. The gun was in a clip holster under the left armpit of the corpse.

Inside the Greek's coat lining was a panel, four inches wide, five times as long, a quarter of an inch thick, hard and rigid.

The Greek's wristwatch ticked.

Sail put the business cards and the panel from the coat lining inside his swim trunks, and was down on his knees cleaning his hands with sand when the situation got the best of his stomach. By the time he finished with that, he had sweated profusely and had a headache over the eyes.

He left the Greek on the island.

The water felt cold as he swam back towards the bugeye, keeping in what dark places he could find. The water chill helped the headache.

Having reached the bugeye with the stuff still in his swim trunks, he clung to the bobstay, the chain brace which ran from the bow waterline to the end of the long bowsprit. He blew the brackish bay water off his lips quietly and listened.

There was no sign anywhere that he had been seen or heard.

He made himself sink and began feeling over the parts of the dock which would still be under water at low tide. Everything under water was inches thick with barnacles and oysters.

He found a niche that would do, took the stuff out of his trunks and wedged it there tightly enough so that there was not much danger of it working out.

Sail clung to the bugeye's bobstay until all the water ran off him that wanted to run, then scrambled aboard and ducked into the cabin.

He had started to shed the bathing suit when the woman said, "Puh-lease!"

Sail came up straight and his head thumped a ceiling carlin.

She swung her legs off the forward bunk. Even then, light from the kerosene gimbal lamp did not reach more than her legs. The feet were small in dark blue sandals which showed red enameled toenails. Her legs had not been shaved recently, and were nice.

Sail chewed an imaginary something between two eye-teeth while he squinted at the girl. He felt of his head where it had hit the ceiling. Two or three times, he seemed about to say something, but didn't and went forward into one of the pair of small single staterooms. The shadow-embedded rest of her did not look bad as he passed.

He shut the stateroom door and got out of the swim trunks. He tied a three-pound fish sinker to the trunks and dropped them through a porthole into the bay, which was dredged three fathoms deep here. He put on his scrubbed dark polo and dungarees.

The girl had moved into the light when he opened the door and entered the cabin. The rest of her was interesting. Twenty something, he judged.

She smiled and said, "You don't act as if you remember me, Wesley."

Sail batted his eyes at her.

"Gosh," she said, "but you're tall!"

Sail scratched behind his right ear, changed his eyebrows

around at her, gave the top of his head three hard rubs, then leaned back against the galley sink. This upset a round bottle. He caught it, looked at it, and seemed to get an idea.

He asked, "Drink?"

She had crossed her legs. Her skirt was split. "That would be nice," she smiled.

Sail, his back to her, made more noise than necessary in rattling bottles and glasses and pinking an opener into a can of condensed milk. He mixed two parts of gin, one of creme de cocoa, one of condensed milk. He put four drops from a small green bottle in one drink and gave that one to the girl, holding it out a full arm length, as if bashful.

They sipped.

"It's not bad without ice, Wesley," she murmured.

Sail said, "Thanks, lady," politely.

Her blue handbag started to slip out of the hollow of her crossed legs and she caught it quickly.

"For a husband, you're a darn polite cuss," she said.

Sail swallowed with a distinctly pigeon noise. "Eh?"

"My Gawd, don't you *remember?*"

"What?"

"If this isn't something! Two weeks ago Tuesday. Four o'clock in the morning. We were pretty tight, but we found a justice of the peace in Cocoanut Grove. You had to hock the engagement ring with the jeep for his fee and twenty dollars, and we all went out and had some drinks, and I kind of lost track of things, including you."

"I'll be—" Sail said vaguely.

The girl put her head back and laughed. The mirth did not sound just right.

"I didn't know what to do," she said. "I remembered you said you were a jewelry drummer out of Cincinnati. I sat around the hotel. Then I began to get a mad up."

An unnaturalness was growing in her voice. She pinched her eyes shut and shook her head. Her blue purse slid to the floor.

"I'm here to tell you I had a time locating you," she said. "I might have known you would be a sailor. Gawd, imagine! Anyway, Mama is right on deck now, Mister, and I want something done about it. If you think you're not the man, you're going to have to prove it in a big way."

"You want me to prove my name, business and recent whereabouts? Is that it?"

"You bet."

Sail said, "That's what I figured."

She peered at him, winking both eyes. Then fright grabbed her face.

"You ain't so damn' smart!" she said through her teeth.

She started to get up, but something was wrong with her knee joints by now, and she slid off the bench and sat hard on the black battleship linoleum.

Sail moved fast and got his long fingers on the blue purse as she clawed it open. A small bright revolver fell out of the purse as they had a tug-o'-war over it.

"Blick!" the girl gasped.

BLICK AND A revolver came out of the oilskin locker. The gun was a small bright twin to the girl's. Blick's Panama fell off slick mahogany hair, and disarranged oilskins fell down in the locker behind him. Blick had his lips rolled in until he seemed to have no lips. He looked about old enough to have fought in the last war.

"Want it shot off?" he gritted.

Sail jerked his hand away from the girl's purse as if a bullet were already heading for it. He put his hands up as high as the cabin carlins and ceiling would allow. The upper part of his stomach jumped slightly with each beat of his heart, moving the polo shirt fabric.

The girl started to get up, couldn't. She said, "Blick!" weakly.

Blick, watching Sail, threw at her, "You hadda be a sucker and try that married-when-you-were-tight gag to find out who he is!"

The girl's lips worked with some words before they got out as sounds. "… was—I—know he—doped drink?"

Blick gritted at Sail, "Bud, she's my sis, and if she don't come out of that, I wouldn't wanta be you!"

Sail watched the bright gun. Sweat had come out on his forehead enough to start running.

"She'll be all right," he said.

"What'd you give her?"

"Truth serum."

"You louse! Fat lot of good it'll do you."

Sail said nothing.

Blick ran his eyes up and down Sail, then said, "They sure left the faucet on too long when they poured you, didn't they, bud?"

Sail got his grin to operate. He said, "Let's see if some words will clear this any."

Blick said, "That's an idea, bud. I think I got you figured. You're some guy Andopolis rung in. It was like Andopolis to get himself some help."

"Andopolis was the one who got knifed?" Sail asked.

"You ain't that dumb."

"Was he?"

"Naw. That was Sam, my pal."

Sail rubbed the top of his head. "I'm sort of confused."

"You and us both," Blick said. "We're confused by you. We ain't seen you around before today. But me and Nola and Sam are watching Andopolis, and he starts out on this dock. You're the only boat out here, so it's a cinch he wanted to see you."

"He only made it about half way out the dock," Sail said dryly.

"Sure. Sam headed him off. Sam wanted to talk to Andopolis was all—"

"It wasn't all," Sail drawled. "What Sam really wanted was to make Andopolis tell him something. Andopolis had some information. Sam wanted it. Sam told Andopolis that if he didn't cough up on the spot he would get his entrails shot out, or words to such effect. Sam reached for his gun. But he had made the mistake of not unbuttoning his coat before he started the argument. Andopolis knew exactly where to put a knife. Sam went off the dock after he gave just one yell."

"And that brought the cop."

Sail squinted one eye. Perspiration was stinging it. He echoed, "And that brought the cop."

Blick was holding the gun steady. He said, "Andopolis ran before the cop got here. He hid in the park and Nola and I tried to get him later, but he broke away and ran."

"Then you came here."

Blick grinned thinly. "Let's get back to the time between the knifing of Sam and the arrival of the cop. You, bud, done some fast work. You were sweet, what I mean. You got a hook and line, grabbed a live fish out of your live-box, jumped on the dock and butchered the fish to hide the marks where Sam got it. You even got the insides of the fish into the water to hide any bloodstains where Sam sank. Then you fed the cop a line when he got there."

"You sure had your eyes open," Sail said.

"Did the cop go for your story?"

"I'm still wondering," Sail said thoughtfully.

BLICK WATCHED SAIL. "How much do you know?"

Sail got rid of his made grin. "I'll bite. How much?"

"So you're going to start that," Blick said.

Nola was breathing noisily. Blick pointed at her, said, "Help me get her going!"

Sail grasped the girl and lifted her.

"Stay that way," Blick ordered, then searched Sail, found no weapon, and said, "Out."

Sail walked the girl up the companionway and on to the dock, then started to let go the girl and get back aboard.

"Along with us," Blick ordered. "It'd be swell if Andopolis has told you what we're trying to find out, wouldn't it?"

Sail said nothing. His breathing was as audible as the girl's. Blick got on the other side of the girl and helped hold her up.

"We're tight," Blick said. "Stagger."

They staggered along the dock to the walk, and along that.

Yacht sailors stood in a knot at the end of the Pier Six lunch stand, and out of the knot came the chug of the slot machines. Blick put his hand and small revolver into a coat pocket. They turned to the right, away from the lunch stand.

Sail said, "You might have the wrong idea about me."

"We'll go into that, bud," Blick said. "We'll go into that in a nice place I know about."

They scuffed over the sidewalk and Blick, walking as if he did not feel as if he weighed more than a ton, seemed to think of a possibility which pleased him.

"Hell, Nola! This guy covered up that knifing for Andopolis, so he's got to be with Andopolis all the way."

Nola did not answer. She was almost sound asleep. Blick pinched her, slapped her, and that awakened her somewhat.

A police radio car was parked at the corner of Biscayne Boulevard and the street they were traveling. Blick did not see it in time. When he did discover it, he took his breath in with a sharp noise.

"We're drunk," Blick warned. "Taking each other home."

Sail shoved a little to steer the girl to the side of the walk farthest from the prowl car. Blick shoved back to straighten them up. He also got mad.

Blick's gun was in his coat pocket, and if shooting started, it was no time for a gun to be in a pocket. Blick started to take it out, probably intending to hold it at his side where it could not be seen from the police car.

Sail watched the gun start out of the pocket. It had a high front sight and there was an even chance of it hanging on the pocket lining. It did.

Sail shoved Blick and Nola as hard as he could. Force of the effort bounced him toward the police car. He grabbed the spare tire at the back of the machine and used it to help himself around.

A policeman in the car yelled, "What the hell's this?" He wasn't excited.

Blick did not shoot. He got Nola over a shoulder and ran. A taxicab was on its stand at the corner. Blick made it.

Sail shouted, "Kidnapers!"

One of the cops leaned out, looked at him, said, "Huh?"

Blick leaped into the taxi with his sister. An instant later, the hack driver fell out of his own machine, holding his head. The taxi took off.

"They stole my heap!" the taxi-driver shrieked.

The police car starter began whining. It whined and whined and nothing happened. One cop wailed, "It never done this before!"

"Try turning on the switch!" Sail yelled.

The motor started.

An officer stuck his head out of the car, said, "You stick around here, wise guy!" and the machine left in pursuit of the cab.

Sail, who had the legs for it, ran away from there very fast.

SAIL, WHEN HE reached the Pier Six lunch stand, planted his hip against the counter, and caught up with his breathing. A young man who looked as youths in lunch stands somehow always look came over, swiped at the counter with his towel, got a look at Sail, blinked and wanted to know, "How's the weather up there?"

"Dry," Sail said. "What you got in cans?"

Sail drank the first and second cans of beer in gulps, but did some pondering over the third. When it was down, he absent-mindedly put three dimes on the counter.

"Forty-five," the youth corrected. "Cans is fifteen."

Sail substituted a half dollar and put the nickel change in one of the slot machines, still involved with his thoughts. The one-armed bandit gave him a lemon and two bars, another bar just showing.

"Almost a jackpot," someone said.

"History," Sail said, "repeating itself."

A telephone booth was housed at the end of Pier Four. Sail dialed the 0 and asked for Police Headquarters.

The slot machines chugged at the lunch stand while he waited. A card on the phone box told how to report a fire, get the police or call an ambulance. He read part of it, and Headquarters answered.

Sail said, "I want to report an attempted robbery. This is Captain Oscar Sail of the yacht *Sail*. A few minutes ago, a man and a woman boarded my boat and marched me away at the point of a gun. I do not know why. I feel they intended to kill me. There was a police car parked at the corner of Biscayne, and I broke away. The man and woman fled in a taxi. The officers chased them. I do not know whether the officers have reported yet."

"They have."

"Did they catch the pair?"

"No."

Sail almost said that was what he had called to find out, but caught himself in time.

"It might help if you described the pair," the police voice said.

Sail described an imaginary couple that were not like Blick and Nola in any particular except that they were man and woman.

"Thanks," said the voice at Headquarters. "When you get aboard your boat, tell Patrolman Joey Cripp to give us a ring. I'm Captain Rader. You'll probably find Patrolman Cripp on your boat."

Sail was wearing a startled look as he hung up and felt for a nickel in the coin return cup of the telephone.

THREE MEN WERE waiting in the cabin of *Sail* when Sail got there. Two wore police uniforms, the other had civilian clothes.

One policeman was using his tongue to lather a new cigar with saliva. The tongue was coated. His neck had some loose red skin on it. He was shaking, not very much, but shaking.

The second officer was the young small patrolman. He still had his flashlight.

The man in civilian clothes was putting bottles and test tubes in a scuffed leather bag which held more of the same stuff and a microscope off which much of the enamel had been worn. His suit was fuzzy gray, rimless spectacles were pinched tight on his nose, and he had chewed half of the cigar in his mouth without lighting it. The cigar was the same kind the policeman with the shakes was licking.

Sail said, "Captain Rader wants Patrolman Joey Cripp to call him."

"That's me," the young patrolman said, and started for the companionway.

"Wait a minute," Sail said. "You didn't happen to get a look at a man and a woman who left here with me a while ago?"

"I sure did. I was behind a bush in the park." The young officer went out.

The shaking policeman got up slowly, holding his damp cigar and looking miserable. He took a full breath and started words coming.

"Gracious but you're a tall man," he said. "I'm Captain Cripp and Joey is my son. This is Mister Waterman. You have a wonderful boat here. Some day I am going to get me a boat like this and go to the South Seas. I want to thank you for reporting your trouble to Captain Rader, which I presume you have just done. And I want to congratulate you on your narrow escape from those two. But next time, don't take such chances. Never fool with a man with a gun. We'll let you know as soon as we hear anything of your attacker and his companion. They got away from the radio car. I hope you have a good time in Miami, and no more trouble. We have a wonderful city, a wonderful climate." He shook with his chill.

Captain Cripp pulled out another cigar and a shiny cylindrical metal lighter. He took another breath.

"Smoke? Of course you do. Better light it yourself. I shake like a leaf. I've got the damned malaria, and every other day, I shake. That's an excellent cigar, if I do say so myself. One of our native products. Made right here in Miami, and as mild as an old maid's kiss. There! Didn't I tell you it was a good cigar?"

He took back his lighter. He did not touch the bright metal where Sail had held it and made fingerprints.

"Isn't admission charged to this?"

"Eh? Oh, yes, you are naturally puzzled by your presence here. Forget it. It means nothing at all. It's just an idea Captain Rader got after talking to Joey about a yell and a fish."

Patrolman Joey Cripp jumped aboard and came below.

"Captain Rader offers his apologies for sending us aboard your boat in your absence," Joey said. "And he wonders if you have anything you would like to say to us."

Sail, his scowl getting blacker and blacker, gritted, "I'm making an effort not to say it!"

Joey said, "Well, Mister Sail, if you will excuse me, we will be going."

The rabbity man, Waterman, finished putting things in his

bag and picked up a camera with a photoflash attachment, pointed the camera at Sail. The outfit clicked and flashed.

"Thank you," he said, not very politely.

They left.

Sail threw the cigar overboard, then examined the cabin. Almost everything had been put back in place carefully. But in one spot, he found fingerprint powder enough to show they had printed the place.

SAIL TRIED TO sleep the rest of the night. He did get a little. The rest of the time he spent at the companion with a mirror which he had rigged on the tip joint of a fishing rod so as to look around without showing himself.

Boats at a slip do not usually have an anchor watch. But on a big Matthews at the opposite slip, somebody seemed to be standing at anchor. The watcher did not smoke, did not otherwise allow any light to get to his features. He might have been tall or short, wide or narrow. The small things he did were what any man would do during a long tiresome job.

There was one exception. The watcher frequently put a finger deep in his mouth and felt around.

Sail took a shower with the dock hose. It gave him a chance to get a better look at the Matthews. The watcher of the night was not in evidence.

The *Sail's* dinghy rode in stern davits, bugeye fashion, at enough of a tilt not to hold spray. Sail lowered it. He got a brush and the dock hose and washed down the black topsides, taking off dried salt which sea water had deposited. He dropped his brush in the water at different times. In each case, it sank, and he had to reach under for it.

The fourth time he reached under for the brush, he retrieved the stuff which he had taken off the Greek. The articles had not worked out of the niche between the dock cross braces under water, where he had jammed them.

Sail finished washing down, hauled the dink up on the davits, and during the business of coiling the dock hose around its faucet, looked around. Any of a dozen persons in sight might have been the watcher off the Matthews. The others would be tourists down for a gawk at the yachts.

He spirited the Greek's stuff below with the scrub brush.

One of the cards said Captain Santorin Gura Andopolis of the yacht *Athens Girl* chartered for Gulf Stream fishing, nobody catching more fish. The address was Pier Five.

The other twenty-six cards said Captain Sam Dokomos owned the Lignum Vitae Towing Company. An address and a telephone number for day calls only.

There was also a piece of board four by twenty inches, a quarter of an inch thick, mahogany, with screw holes in four corners. The varnish was peeled, rather than worn, as was some of the gold leaf. The gold leaf formed a letter, four figures.

K 9420

Sail burned everything in the galley Shipmate.

There was no one in the telephone booth at the end of the pier. He looked up the number of Pier Five, which was no more than two hundred feet distant, and dialed it.

"Captain Andopolis," he requested.

Through the window, he could see them go looking for Captain Andopolis. It took them almost five minutes to decide they couldn't find him.

"Maybe he went to the dentist, somebody thought," the one who had hunted suggested.

"Yeah?"

"Yeah. He's been having a toothache, somebody said."

Sail went back to the bugeye and put on a dark suit, tropical weight, a black polo shirt and black shoes. His shore cruising rig.

THE CAFETERIA WAS overdone in chromium. The darkies who carried the trays were dressed in the same red that was on the walls. There were a score of customers and a boy who wandered among the tables selling newspapers and racing dope sheets. He sold more dope sheets than papers.

One man eating near the door did not put syrup on his pancakes or sugar in his coffee. When he finished, he put a finger in the back of his mouth to feel.

Sail finished his beer and doughnuts and strolled around the corner to a U-Drive-It.

The only car on which they did not want a deposit was a little six-cylinder sedan, not new. Sail drove it around, sticking his head out frequently to look for a tall building. He found it and parked in front of it.

He made a false start into the building, then came back to take another look at an upright dingus. Then he went inside.

He told the elevator operator loudly, "Five!" before they started up.

The fifth floor corridor was empty.

When the man who had felt of his tooth in the cafeteria came sneaking up the stairs, Sail was set. He had his belt strapped tight around his fist. The man got down on all fours to mew his pain. Sail hit again, then unwrapped the belt, blew on his fist, worked the fingers.

He had the senseless man in his arms when the elevator answered his signal.

"Quick! I gotta rush my friend to a place for a treatment!" he explained.

He drove five or six miles on a side road off the Tamiami Trail before he found a lonesome spot and got out. He hauled the man out.

The man began big at the top and tapered. His small hands were calloused, dirt was ground into the callouses, the nails broken. His face was darker than his hair.

A leather envelope purse held three hundred in old and new bills. There was a dollar sixty-one in change and the cashier's slip for his cafeteria breakfast in his trousers.

A knife was in a holster against the small of his back. It was flat and supported by a high belt. Sail threw it in the canal at the roadside. It was not the one with which he had knifed Sam. He had left that one in his victim.

Handfuls of water from the canal did not speed his revival much. When he finally came around, he groaned, squirmed, and started feeling of his bad tooth.

Sail stood back and showed him a fat blue revolver. "Just try to be nonchalant, Andopolis," he advised.

Andopolis immediately stood up.

"Sit down!" Sail directed sharply.

Andopolis walked towards him.

Sail shoved the gun out, gritting desperately, "This thing is loaded, you fool!"

Andopolis leaped. Sail dodged, but hardly enough. Andopolis hit him with a shoulder. The impact spun him. Since he didn't want to shoot, the gun was a handicap. It tied up his fists. Andopolis hit him on the belt buckle. Numbness grabbed the whole front of his body. Something suddenly against his back was the ground.

"Yah!" Andopolis screeched. "Yah!"

He jumped, feet together, at Sail's middle. Sail was too numb to move clear. The feet hit his chest, everything seemed to break, and red-hot pain knocked the numbness out. Sail got Andopolis' legs, jerked. Andopolis windmilled his arms, but fell.

Sail clamped on to one of the man's feet and began doing things to it and the leg. Andopolis, turning over and over, raised a dust cloud. He moaned and bellowed and made dog noises. Where he judged Andopolis was dizzy enough, Sail pounced on the dust cloud. He hit, variously, an arm, the ground, a hip, and other places which he could not identify.

Andopolis, bewildered and with dirt in his eyes, failed to get his jaw out of the way.

SAIL STRAIGHTENED, PUT back his head and started to take a full breath. He began coughing. Hacking, gagging, holding his chest, he sat down in the road. He began to sweat profusely. After a while, he unbuttoned his pants and pulled up his shirt. There was one purple print of the entire bottom of both of Andopolis' feet, and the chest was skinned, the loose skin mixed with the long golden hair. There was not much blood.

Andopolis got his eyes open and snarled, "Yah! I stomp you good if you don't lay off me!"

Sail coughed and got up. He kept his feet far apart, but did not teeter much.

He said thickly, "My Macedonian friend, you stood anchor watch on me all night and you were still trailing me this morning. Where do you get that lay off stuff?"

"Before that, I'm talk about," Andopolis growled.

"Eh?"

Andopolis took a breath and blew words out. "For two week now, you been follow me like dog. I go to Bimini two day, and you and that black bugeye in Bimini before long. I make the run from Bimini here yesterday. You make him too. Vat you take me for? One blind owl, huh?"

Sail asked, "Do you think you're bulletproof, too?"

Andopolis snorted. "Me, I don't theenk you shoot."

"What gave you that idea?"

"Go jump in hell," Andopolis said.

Sail coughed some, deep and low, trying to keep it from moving his ribs.

He said, "All right, now that we're being honest with each other, I'll tell you a true story about a yacht named *Lady Luck*. That's just so there won't be any misunderstanding about who knows what."

Andopolis crowded his lips into a bunch and pushed the bunch out as far as he could, but didn't say anything.

Sail began:

"The *Lady Luck*, Department of Commerce registration number K 9420, was as neat a little yacht as ever kedged off Featherbed Bank. She belonged to Bill Lord of Tulsa. Oil. Out in Tulsa, they call Bill the Osage Ogre, on account of he's got what it seems to take to find oil. Missus Bill likes jewelry, and Bill likes her, so he buys her plenty. Because Missus Bill really likes her rocks, she carries them around with her. You following me?"

Andopolis was. He still had his lips pursed.

"Bill Lord had his *Lady Luck* anchored off the vet camp on Lower Matecumbe last November," Sail continued. "Bill and the Missus were ashore, looking over the camp. Bill was in the trenches himself, back when, and is some kind of a shot in the American Legion or the Democrats, so he was interested in the camp. The Missus left her pretties on the yacht. Remember that. Everybody has read about the hurricane that hit that afternoon, and maybe some noticed that Bill and his Missus were among those who hung on behind that tank car. But the *Lady Luck* wasn't so lucky, and she dragged her picks off somewhere and sank. For a while, nobody knew where."

Sail stopped to cough. He had to lie down on his back before he could stop, and he was very careful about getting erect again. Perspiration had wet most of him.

He said, "A couple of weeks ago, a guy asked the Department of Commerce lads to check and give him the name of the boat, and the name of the owner, that carried the number K 9420. That was the mistake."

"Pooey," Andopolis said, "on your story."

"The word got to me," Sail continued. "Never mind how. And it was easy to find you were the lad asking for the dope on K 9420. Inquiry brought out that you had had a fishing party down around Matecumbe and Long Key a few days before you suddenly got curious about K 9420. It was a little harder to locate the parties who had your boat hired at the time. Two Pan-American pilots. They said you anchored off Lower Matecumbe to bottom fish, and your anchor fouled something, and you had a time, and finally, when you got the anchor up, you brought aboard some bow planking off a sunken boat. From the strain as it was torn loose, it was apparent the anchor had pulled the planking off the rest of the boat, which was still down there. You checked up as a matter of course to learn what boat you had found."

Andopolis looked as if something besides his tooth hurt him.

"Tough you didn't get in touch with the insurance people instead of contacting Captain Sam Dokomas, a countryman of yours who had a towing and salvage outfit, and a bad reputation."

Andopolis growled, "Damn! You said somethin' then!"

Sail kept his voice lower to decrease the motion of his ribs in expelling air for words. "You needed help to get the *Lady Luck*. But Captain Sam Dokomas tried to make you cough up the exact location. Then you smelled a doublecross, got scared and lit for Bimini.

"I had been hanging around all this time, and not doing a good job of it, so you got wise to me. That scared you back to Miami. You had decided on a showdown, and were headed for my boat when Captain Sam collared you on the dock. You took care of part of your troubles with a knife right there. But that left Captain Sam's girl friend and her brother, Blick, and Nola, or whatever their names are. They were in the know. They tried to grab you in the park after you fixed Sam up, but you outran them.

"Now, that's a very complete story, don't you think? Oh, yes. You got reckless and jumped me a minute ago because you figured I wouldn't shoot you because nobody but you knows the exact location of the *Lady Luck*. The two Pan-American boys fishing down there with you when you found the ship forgot to take bearings and didn't have a smell of an idea where they were at the time."

Andopolis was a man who did his thinking with the help of his face, and there was more disgust than anything else on his features.

"YOU TRYING TO cut in?" he snarled finally.

"Not trying. Have."

Andopolis thought that over. The sun was comfortable, but mosquitoes were coming out of the swamp around the road to investigate, hungrier than land sharks.

"Yeah," Andopolis muttered finally. "I guess you have, at that."

"Let's get this straight, Andy. You and I, and nobody else."

Andopolis nodded. "O.K."

"Now just who is this Blick?"

"Nola's brother."

"Now, hell, Andy—"

"And Nola was married to that double-crosser, Sam."

Sail made a whistling mouth. "So it was Nola's husband you dirked. She'll like you for that."

"So what? She didn't go for him much."

"No?"

"Naw. That dame—"

"Skip it," Sail said suddenly. He put his shirt on, favoring his chest. "Dang, feller, you sure busted up my ribs. We've got to watch the insurance company. They paid off on Missus Bill's stuff. Over a hundred thousand. They'll have wires out."

Andopolis nodded. "What about stuff for diving?"

"There's sponger equipment aboard my bugeye," Sail said. "I tried that racket over in Tarpon Springs, but you can't compete with those Greeks over there."

"Let's go," Andopolis said.

He was feeling of his tooth when he got in the car. Sail drove slowly. The road, nothing more than a high dike built up with material scooped out to make the drainage canal, was rough. It hurt his ribs.

Sail had driven no more than half a mile when both front tires let go their air. Maybe the car would still have remained on the road. But bullets also knocked holes in the windshield. The car was in the canal before anything could be done about it.

THE CAR BROKE most of its windows going down the canal bank. The canal must have been six feet deep. Its tea-colored water filled the machine at once. Sail's middle hurt, and he had lost his air, and had to breathe in, and there was nothing but water.

After the water had filled the car, it seemed to rush around inside. Sail tried the doors, but they wouldn't open. He did not touch Andopolis in his struggles. Andopolis did not seem to be in the car. Sail couldn't remember him having been thrown out.

The first window Sail found was too small. He pummeled the car roof, but hardly had strength enough to knock himself away from what he was hitting. Then he was suddenly out of the car. He didn't know just how he had managed it. He reached the top, but sank twice before he clutched a weed on shore, after which an attack of the spasms kept him at first from hearing the shots.

Yells were mixed in the shot noise. Sail squeezed water off his eyeballs with the lids, looked, and saw Andopolis on the canal bank. Andopolis was some distance away and running madly.

Blick and his sister Nola were running after Andopolis. They were shooting at Andopolis' legs, it seemed.

They all three ran out of sight, but the sounds told Sail they had winged Andopolis and grabbed him.

Sail had wrenched some of the water out of his lungs by now. He swam to a bush which hung down into the water and got under it. He managed to get his coughing stopped.

Andopolis was sobbing at the top of his voice when Blick and Nola dragged him up.

"Shoot his other leg off if he acts up, Nola," Blick said. "I'll get our tall bud."

Sail began to want to cough. He desired the cough until it was almost worth getting shot for.

"He must be a submarine," Blick said. He got a stick and poked around. "Hell, Nola, this water is eight feet deep here anyhow."

Andopolis bubbled something in Greek.

"Shut up," Blick said, "or we'll put bullets into you like we put 'em into the tires of your car."

Andopolis went on bubbling.

"His leg is bleeding bad, Blick," Nola said.

"Hell I care! He knifed your husband, didn't he?"

Air kept coming up in big bubbles from the submerged car. Sail tried to keep his mind off the cough. Blick stood for a century on the bank with his bright little pistol.

"He musta drowned," Blick said.

Andopolis moaned.

"Didn't you know we had been shaggin' you all night and mornin'?" Blick asked him. "Hell, if you hadn't been so occupied with that long lean punk, you'd have got wise, maybe."

Nola said, "We better get his leg fixed."

"If he ain't free with his information, he won't need his leg any more," Blick said. "Let's get the hell away from here."

Andopolis whimpered as they hazed him away. They apparently had a car in the bushes beside the canal some distance down the road. Its noise went away. Sail crawled out and had a good cough.

CAPTAIN CRIPP LOOKED wide-eyed and hearty and without a sign of a chill as he exclaimed, "Well, well, good morning, good morning. You know, we began to think something had happened to you."

Sail looked at him with eyes that appeared to be drained of everything but the will to carry on, then stumbled down the remaining three steps into the main cabin of *Sail*. He let himself down on the starboard seat. Pads of cotton under gauze thickened his neck and wrists. He had discovered the car windows had cut him. Iodine had run from under one of the pads and dried. He had just come from the hospital.

Young bony Patrolman Joey Cripp looked at Sail. His grin took the looseness out of the corner of his mouth.

"Tsk, tsk," he said. "Now that's terrible. You look a sight. By God, it's a wonder you're alive. I hope that didn't happen in Miami."

Sail gave them a look of bile. "This is a private boat, in case you forgot."

"Now, now, I hope we can keep things on an amiable footing," Captain Cripp murmured.

Sail said, "Drag it!" His face was more cream than any other color. He reached behind himself in the tackle locker and got a gaff hook. A four-foot haft of varnished oak with a tempered bright steel hook of needle point. He showed them the hook and his front teeth. "I've got a six-aspirin headache, and things to go with it! You two polite public servants get out of here before I go fishing for kidneys!"

Patrolman Joey Cripp stood up. "I didn't think we'd have any trouble with you, Mister Sail. I hoped we wouldn't, on account of you acted like a gentleman last night."

"Sit the hell down, Joey," Captain Cripp put in. "Mister Sail, you're under arrest, I'm sorry to say."

Sail said, "Arrest?" He scowled. "Is this on the level?"

"It sure is."

"Pop said it," agreed young Joey.

Captain Cripp shook a finger at Sail. He said:

"Listen. Waterman found human blood in that fish mess on the dock last night. The harbor squad's diver went down this morning. He found a bathing suit with a sinker tied to it. He also found a live box with some live barracuda in it. It was a barracuda you butchered on the dock. Your fishline you had in your hand when Joey got there was wet, but it don't take a minute to wet a line. You described a man and a woman that looked a lot different from the pair Joey saw you with. We been doing some arithmetic, and we figure you were covering up."

"Now," Sail said, "I guess I'm supposed to get scared?"

"I don't know," Captain Cripp said, "but a dead Greek was found over on the island this morning. And in your bathing suit which the diver got was some island sand, and some stickers off the pine trees like grows on the island."

"I guess," Joey said, "it does look kinda funny."

"I regret that it does," Captain Cripp agreed. "After all, evidence is evidence, and while Miami has a wonderful hospitality, we do draw lines, and when our visitors go so far as to use knives on—"

"Let's get this straight!" Sail put in. "Pine tree stickers and sand are just about alike here and in Key West, and points between."

"You may be assured—"

Sail sprang up gripping the hook. He began to yell.

"What's the idea of this clowning? I know two lug cops when I see 'em. If you got something to say, get it off your chests."

Joey sighed. "I guess courtesy is somethin' you can't acquire. Whatcha say, Pop? Hell with the chief's courtesy campaign, huh?"

"Now that you mention it, Joey, O.K." Captain Cripp pulled manacles out of his hip pocket. "We're gonna fan you into the can, and we're gonna work you over until we get the straight of this."

Sail slammed the gaff into a corner.

"That's more like. If you hadn't tried to fancy pants around last night, I'd have showed you something then."

Sail shuffled into the galley and got the rearmost can of beer out of the icebox. It gurgled when he shook it, but that was because of the small sealed jar of water which fitted inside it. Stuffed around the jar were some sheets of paper. He held the documents out to the two policemen.

Joey raked his eyes over the print and penned signatures, then spelled them out, lips moving.

"Aw, this don't make no difference," he said. "Or does it?"

Captain Cripp complained, "My glasses fell off yesterday when I was having one of my infernal chills. What does it say, Joey?"

"He's a private dick commissioned to locate some stuff that sank on a yacht called the *Lady Luck*. The insurance people hired him."

CAPTAIN CRIPP BUTTONED his coat, squared it over his hips, set his cap with a pat on the top. "Who signed the papers, Joey?"

Joey said, "They're all right, Pop. From what it says, I guess this private op is the head of something called Marine Investigations. Reckon that's an agency, huh?"

Captain Cripp sighed and ambled over to the companionway. "Beauty before age, Joey."

Joey bristled. "Shamus or no shamus, I say it don't make no difference!"

"Let the next guy have the honor, Joey."

"Look, Pop, damn it—"

"The last private op I worked over got me two years in the sticks. He said something about me chiseling in on the reward, and the skipper believed him. It was a damned lie, except—well—out, Joey."

"But Pop, this stinker—"

"Out!" Captain Cripp barked. "You're as big a fool as your maw!"

Joey licked his lips, raking Sail with malevolent eyes. Then he turned and climbed the companion steps.

Captain Cripp looked at Sail. He felt for the bottom step with one foot without looking down. As if he didn't expect it to do any good, he asked, "You wouldn't want to cooperate?"

"I wouldn't."

"Why not?"

"I've done it before."

Captain Cripp grinned slightly. "Just as you say. But if you get yourself in a sling, it'd be better if you had a reason for refusing to help the police."

"All I get out of this is ten per cent for recovering the stuff. I can't see a split. I need the dough."

"And you with a boat like this."

"Maybe I like boats and maybe it keeps me broke."

"The only reason you're not in the can right now is that any shyster could make this circumstantial evidence look funny as hell. Forget the split."

"Thanks," Sail said. "Now I'm going to sound off. It just might be that you lads think you can let me finish it out, then step in, and maybe find the location of that boat for yourselves. Then, while I was in your bastille, trying to explain things you could think to ask me, the stuff might disappear off the boat."

"That's kind of plain talk."

"I feel kind of plain right now."

Captain Cripp's ears moved up a little with the tightening of his jaw muscles. He took his foot off the companion step. He gave his cap an angry adjustment. Then he put the foot back again.

"This malaria is sure something. I feel like a lark today, only I keep thinking about the chills tomorrow."

"Try whiskey and quinine," Sail said.

"I think the whiskey part gave it to me."

The two cops went away with Joey kicking his feet down hard at the dock planks.

Sail took rye and aspirin for what ailed him, changed clothes, took a taxi uptown and entered what looked like the largest hardware store. He asked where they kept their marine charts.

THE NERVOUS OLD salesman in the chart department had a rip in his canvas apron. He mixed his talk in with waving gestures of a pipe off which most of the stem had been chewed.

"Mister, you must have some funny things happen to you, you being so tall," he said. "Right now, you look as if you had had an accident."

Sail steadied himself by holding to the counter edge. "Who sells government charts here, Dad?"

"Well, there's one other store besides us. Hopkins Carter. But if you're going down in the Keys, we got everything you need here. If you go inside, you'll want charts thirty-two-sixty and sixty-one. They're the strip charts. But if you take Hawk Channel, you'll need harbor chart five-eighty-three, and charts twelve-forty-nine, fifty and fifty-one. Here, I'll show—"

Sail squinted his eyes, swallowed, and said, "I don't want to buy a chart. I want you to slip out and telephone me if either of a certain two persons comes in here and asks for chart twelve-fifty, the one which covers Lower Matecumbe."

"Huh?"

Sail said patiently, "It's easy, Dad. You just tell the party you got to get the chart, and go telephone me. Then stall around three or four minutes as if you were getting the chart out of the stock room. That will give me time to get over here and pick up their trail."

The nervous old man put his pipe in his mouth and immediately took it out again. "What kind of shenanygin is this?"

Sail showed him a license to operate in Florida.

"One of them fellers, huh?" The old man did not seem impressed.

Sail put a five-dollar bill on the counter. "That one's got a twin. How about it?"

The old man picked up the bill, squinted at it. "You mean this is a counterfeit or something. What—"

"No, no, control your imagination, Dad. The five is good, and it's yours, and another one like it, if you help me."

"You mean I keep this whether they show up or not?"

"That's the idea."

"Go ahead, Mister, and describe them people."

Sail made a word picture of Blick and Nola. Not trusting Dad's memory, he put the salient points down on a piece of paper. He added a telephone number. "That phone is a booth in a cigar store on the next corner. How far is this Hopkins Carter store?"

" 'Bout two blocks, I reckon."

"I'll be there for the next ten minutes. Then I'll be in the cigar store. Ask for Chief Steward Johnson, when you call."

"That you?"

"Uh-huh."

Sail, walking off, was not as pale as he had been on the boat. He had put on a serge suit with more black than blue and a new black polo. When he was standing in front of the elevator, taking a pull at a flat amber bottle which had a crown and a figure on the label, the old man yelled, "Mister!"

Sail lowered the bottle, started coughing.

"Lemme look at this again and see if you said anything about the way he talked," the old man said.

Sail moved back to where he could see the old fellow peering at the paper which held the descriptions. The old man took his pipe out of his teeth. "Mister, what does that feller talk like?"

"Well, about like the rest of these crackers. No, wait. He'll call you bud two or three times."

The old man waved his pipe. "I already sold that man a twelve-fifty."

"The hell!"

"Around half an hour ago, I reckon."

"That's swell!" Sail pumped air out of his lungs in a short laugh which had no sound except such noise as the air made going past his teeth and out of his nostrils. "There was this one chance. They would probably want a late chart for their X-marks-the-spot. And now they've got it, so they'll be off to the wars." He kissed a palm sneeringly. "That for the whole works!"

He weaved around, a lot more unsteady than he had been a minute before. He put the flat flask between his teeth and looked at the spinning ceiling fan. By the time the bottle was empty, his head and eyes were screwing around in time with the fan blades. He got his feet tracking in the general direction of the door.

The old man said, "That there chart was delivered."

Sail maneuvered a turn and halt. "Eh?"

"He ordered it over the telephone, and we delivered. I got the address somewhere." The old man thumbed his order book, stopping to point at each name with his pipe stem.

"Whileaway," he said finally. "A houseboat on the Miami River below the Twelfth Street Causeway."

Sail cocked the empty bottle in a wastebasket, put five dollars in front of the old man and headed for the elevator. He was a lot steadier.

THE HOUSEBOAT *WHILEAWAY* was built for rivers, and not very wide ones. Sixty feet or thereabouts waterline, she had three decks that put her up like a skyscraper. She was white, or had been. A man who loved boats would have said she should never have been built.

Scattered on shore near was a gravel pile, two trucks with nobody near them, a shed, junk from the hurricane, a trailer with both tires flat and windows broken, and two rowboats in as bad shape as the trailer.

Sail was behind most of the junk at one time or another on his way to the river bank. The river ran between wooden bulkheads at this point. Between Sail and *Whileaway*, two tugs, a yawl, a cruiser and another houseboat were tied to dolphins along the bulkhead. Nobody seemed to be on any of the boats.

Sail stripped to dark blue silk underwear shorts. He hid everything else under the junk. The water had a little more smell and floating things than in the harbor. After he had eased down into it, he kept behind the moored boats, next to the bulkhead. The tide carried him. He was just coming under the bow of *Whileaway* when one of the square window ports of the houseboat opened.

Sail sank suddenly. He thought somebody was going to shoot, or use a harpoon.

Something heavy—evidently it fell out of the porthole—hit the water. It sank quickly. Touching Sail, it pushed him aside. It went on sinking. Sail got the idea that a navy anchor was at the lowermost part of the sinking object.

He swam down after it. The river had only two fathoms here. He did not have much trouble finding it. When he clung to the object, the tide stretched his legs out behind.

Whoever had tied the knots was a sailor. Sailor knots, while they hold, are made to be easily untied. Sail got them loose. He began to think he wouldn't make the top with his burden. He was out of air.

His head came out of the water with eyes open, fixed in the direction of the square port. Nobody's head was there. No weapon appeared.

Sail looked around, then threw an arm up. He missed the first springline which held the houseboat to the bulkhead. He grasped the next one. He held Nola's head out.

Water leaked from Nola's nose and mouth.

Some of the rope which had tied her to the heavy navy anchor was still wrapped around her. Sail used it to tie her to the springline, so that her head was out of the water.

Then he had to try twice before he could get up the springline to the houseboat deck. Nola began gagging and coughing. It made a racket.

Sail stumbled through the handiest door. Waves of pain jumped from his ribs to his toes, from ribs to hair. The bandages had turned red, and it was not from mercurochrome.

THE HOUSEBOAT FURNISHINGS must have been something fifteen years ago. Most of the varnish had alligatored. Sail got into the galley by accident. Rust, dirt, smell. He grabbed the only things in sight, a quart brass fire extinguisher and a rusted ice pick.

He found a dining salon beyond the galley. He was half across it when Andopolis came in the opposite door.

Andopolis had a rusty butcher knife in one hand. He was using the other hand to handle a chair for crutch, riding it with the knee of the leg which Blick and Nola had put a bullet through.

Clustered around Andopolis' eyes—more on the lids than elsewhere—were puffy gray blisters. They were about the size burning cigarettes would make. Two fingernails were off one of his hands, the one which held the butcher knife. Red ran from the mutilated fingertips down over the rusty knife.

Sail threw the fire extinguisher. He was weaker even than he had thought. The best he could do was bounce the extinguisher off the bulkhead behind Andopolis.

Andopolis said thickly, "I feex you up this time, fran!" and reversed the knife for throwing.

Sail threw his ice pick. It was a good shot. The pick stuck into Andopolis' chest over his heart. But it did not go in deep enough to trouble Andopolis. He never bothered to jerk it out. He already had enough pain elsewhere not to know it was there.

Feet banged through the boat behind Sail. They approached.

Andopolis threw. Sail dropped. His weakness seemed to help. The knife went over his head.

A uniformed cop had appeared in the door. Bad luck put him in the path of the knife. He made a bleating sound, took spraddling steps and leaned against a bulkhead, his hands trying to cover the handle of the butcher knife and his left shoulder. He made a poor job of it.

Sail got up and lurched around Andopolis. The chair crutch

made Andopolis clumsy.

Once through the door behind Andopolis, Sail found himself in what had once been the main cabin, and pretended to be, still.

Blick sat on the cabin floor, his face a mess. His visage was smeared with blue ink. The ink bottle was upside down under a table on which a new marine chart was spread open. A common writing pen lay on the chart.

Andopolis came in after Sail, banging on the chair crutch. The ice pick still stuck in his chest by its point. He came at Sail, hopped on one leg, and swung his chair with the other.

Sail, coughing, hurting all over, tried to dodge. He made it, but fell down. Andopolis swung the chair. Sail rolled, and the chair went to pieces on the floor.

Nola was still screaming. Men were swearing outside. More men were running around on the houseboat, trying to find the way below. A police siren was whining.

Andopolis held a leg of his chair still. It was heavy enough to knock the brains out of an ox. He hopped for Sail.

Sail, looking about wildly, saw the fire extinguisher on the floor. It must have bounced in here. Maybe somebody had kicked it in accidentally. He rolled to it.

Andopolis lifted the chair leg.

The extinguisher made *ink-sick!* noises as Sail pumped it. No tetrachloride came out. Nothing happened to indicate it ever would. Then a first squirt ran out about a foot. The second was longer. The third wet Andopolis' chest. Sail aimed and pumped. The tetrachloride got into Andopolis' eyes.

Andopolis made snarling sounds and couldn't see any more.

Sail got up and weaved to the table.

The chart on the table had two inked lines forming a V with arms that ran to landmarks on Lower Matecumbe island in the Florida keys. Compass bearings were printed beside each arm, and the point where the lines came together was ringed.

Several times, Sail's lips moved, repeating the bearings, the landmarks.

Then Sail picked up the pen. He made a NE into a NNE and a SSE out of an E.

His letters looked enough like the others that nobody would guess the difference. And the lines of the V were wavy. They had not been laid out with a protractor from the compass roses. Therefore, they did not indicate an exact spot. Probably they varied as much as a mile, for the *Lady Luck* seemed to lie well off Matecumbe. Nobody would locate any sunken boat from that chart now.

SAIL WAS REPEATING the true bearings to fix them in his memory when Andopolis came hopping in. Andopolis was still blind, still had his chair leg.

Blick, on the floor, called, "Nola—kid—what's—wrong?" He didn't seem to know where he was or what was happening.

Andopolis weaved for Blick's mumbling voice.

"Blick!" Sail yelled thickly. "Jump!"

Blick said foolishly, "Was that—you—Nola?"

Sail was stumbling towards him, fully aware he would not make it in time. He didn't. He woke up nights for quite a while hearing the sound Andopolis' chair leg and Blick's head made.

Andopolis hopped around, still quite blind, and made for Sail. He had his chair leg raised. Hair, blood and brains stuck to the hickory chair leg. Sail got out of the way.

Andopolis stopped, stood perfectly still, and listened. Sail did not move. He was pale, swaying. He squatted, got his hands on the floor, sure he was going to fall if he didn't. He tried not to breathe loudly enough for Andopolis to hear.

Captain Cripp, Patrolman Joey Cripp and the old man from the hardware store came in together looking around.

The old man pointed at Sail and began, "There's the man who asked about the feller that got the chart. I told you I told him the chart was delivered here, and he probably had come right—"

Andopolis rushed the voice, holding his chair leg up.

"Look out!" Sail croaked.

Andopolis instantly veered for where he thought Sail's voice had come from. He was a little wrong. It was hard for him to maintain a direction hopping on one leg. He hopped against a wall. Hard.

Andopolis sighed, leaned over backward and hit the floor. He had a fit. A brief fit, ending by Andopolis straightening out and relaxing. Hitting the wall had driven the ice pick the rest of the way into his chest.

Sail remained on all fours on the floor. He felt, except for the pain, as if he were very drunk on bad liquor. He must have remained on his hands and knees a long time, for he was vaguely aware that Captain Cripp and Joey had walked around and around him, but without speaking. Then they went over to the table and found the chart.

They divided their looking between the chart and each other.

"It's it," Joey said.

"Yeah." Captain Cripp sounded thoughtful. "What about it, Joey?"

"You're the boss, Pop."

Captain Cripp turned the corners of his mouth down. He folded the chart, stuck it inside his clothing, under his belt. Then he straightened his uniform.

A DOCTOR CAME in at last. He seemed to be a very silent doctor. He picked up Andopolis' wrist, held it awhile, then put it back on the floor carefully. The wrist and arm were more flexible than that much rubber would have been. The doctor did not speak.

Sail was still on all fours. The doctor upset him gently. Sail had his tongue between his teeth. The doctor explored with his hands; when he came to Sail's chest, a small amount of sound escaped between Sail's tongue and teeth.

"My God!" the doctor said.

Four men helped with the stretcher as far as the ambulance, but only two when it came to getting the stretcher into the ambulance. Two could manage it better, using a system which they had. The ambulance motor started.

Captain Cripp got into the ambulance with Sail. He was holding his right hand to his nose.

"About Joey," he said. "I been wondering if Joey believed in something on the side, when he could get it. You know, kinda the modern idea."

He took his hand from his nose and quickly put a handkerchief in its place. The handkerchief got red at once.

Then he put the folded marine chart under Sail's head.

"Joey," he chuckled, "is as old-fashioned as angels, only he about busted my beak before I could explain."

Angelfish

Sail faces three hurricanes—a
girl, the wind and killers

SHE WAS A long, blue-eyed girl who lay squarely on her back with the sun shining in her mouth. Her teeth were small and her tongue was flat, not pointed, and there was about two whiskey glassfuls of scarlet liquid in her mouth.

As she turned her head slowly to the side, the scarlet emptied out on the black asphalt walk, splashing her tan columnar neck and the shoulder of her white frock.

Sail stood beside her and kept looking at the gun in his hand. It was a long, black gun. Sail was a long, brown man, dressed in black—black polo shirt, black trousers and black tennis shoes.

They were very alone, the two of them. The sky overhead was queer, with too much clarity in it. There was no air stirring. The palm fronds, the hibiscus leaves all around were as still as if painted on glass. Seagulls in the air were the only moving things. And they were not circling. They were flying silently inland, fleeing from something.

Sail ran thin fingers slowly through his hair and down hard over the back of his neck. Weather and salt water had not left much color in his hair.

The girl coughed, hackingly.

Sail's mouth looked as if he were holding his tongue with his teeth as he bent to get at her brown leather bag. A chain connected the bag to the girl's wrist. The bag was locked, and Sail opened his pocket knife, punctured the bag and made a slit. His long forefinger raked out loose greenbacks, a flat package and a letter of credit which bore the girl's name. Nan Moberly.

The package was not quite as large as a box of kitchen matches. Sail took it and left the other stuff.

Nan Moberly coughed once more.

"Darn it!" she said. "Some of that red stuff went down the wrong way."

Sail said darkly, "I still think this stunt takes the goofy prize."

"I didn't hire you for your advice. I hired you because you are an honest private detective, if there really is such a thing."

"The advice is thrown in. Nobody in his right mind is going to think you've got a bullet in the lung."

"Put some of that red stuff on the bosom of my dress."

Sail did so. The hole was already in her dress. He pocketed the bottle.

She said, "O.K. I've got a doctor hired to swear I've been shot."

"Take some advice, lady. This—"

"Save it." She coughed again, not as hard. "On with the act."

Sail said, "I like to know what I'm mixing in."

"You know what you're getting paid to do. That's enough."

The girl ripped out a long terrible scream.

Sail fired the gun in the air. Its report made the passing gulls dodge wildly. Sail dropped the gun and galloped off, carrying the package.

When he had covered fifty yards, he ducked behind a clump of shrubbery and waited, making a small hole through the leaves so he could watch Nan Moberly. He looked as serious as he could look with such a big mouth. He did not seem to be liking what he was doing.

THE SHRUBBERY WAS thick all around. It was planted shrubbery, but had not been getting much attention. The spot was not a park, but undeveloped real estate in the north end of Miami Beach. A few houses were scattered about. The sidewalk on which the girl lay led to one, the roof of which was visible.

A man came from the house. He was a dark man, not much

more than half as tall as Sail, but very broad. He wore a checked sport coat, a white towel tucked in the collar, and black bathing shorts. His legs were almost black with suntan and built like the front legs of a draft horse.

He reached the girl, stared at her.

"Caesar!" he yelled. "Caesar!"

Another man came loping from the house. A young man in a red bathing suit, very blond, very fat and very blistered by the Florida sun.

Sail made a whistling mouth, but no sound, when he saw the two shiny revolvers the blond man carried.

The blond young man reached Nan Moberly.

"Yay, Sanders!" he boomed. "Nan Moberly!"

Sanders got down on his draft horse knees and jammed a hand into the brown leather bag. He groped in the bag for a moment.

"Somebody hijacked her!" he gritted.

Caesar screeched, "Yee!"

Sail backed away from his hiding place, keeping down. He covered another fifty yards, and by that time he was perspiring and had hold of his lower lip with his teeth. He set himself, but hung on his mark like a sprinter waiting for the gun. Finally, he muttered, "The things some guys do for money!" and launched himself into the open.

Caesar saw him, bawled. Sanders yelled, "He's got it in his hand!"

Caesar's guns scared the seagulls. Sail got behind more brush. And bullets swatted through the leaves ahead of him.

Sail's lips were off his teeth. He breathed hard, although he was not yet winded. With long-legged, desperate haste, he went over everything that was not too high. He came to a long white wall around a house and vaulted into a yard and pounded across it. Two men were nailing boards over the windows of the house and a woman was handing them nails. They stopped work and gaped.

Sail took the other wall, turned his right ankle on one of several coconuts under a palm tree, favored the leg for a few yards, and got speed again. There was a street on the right, and when he saw a taxicab cruising along it, he veered over.

Sail overhauled the cab, opened the door and got in with a radio that was saying, "*—has requested that citizens fasten securely or place in a sheltered spot all loose objects. Another bulletin from this station will follow shortly.*" Music started.

The taxi driver had been listening to that with a rapt grin.

"Swab my deck, mate!" he chortled gleefully. "We're gonna get it! We're gonna get it!"

Sail, leaning forward to tell him where to go, saw a clumsy looking wooden peg-leg lying on the seat beside the driver.

Sail said, "Sail her hard, John Silver. Miami, the nearest way."

The driver said, "John Silver *is* the name, believe it or not."

ALL THE WAY, houses were being shuttered and boards nailed over windows, and an attendant was taking down a swinging sign on a filling station on Biscayne Boulevard. Trucks were peddling lumber from house to house; passenger cars traveling the streets had planks tied on the fenders or sticking out of the windows. Radios in almost every house poured out static noise as if it were broken glass.

"Aye, aye, mate," John Silver chuckled. "I can nearly smell it."

At Biscayne and Miami Avenue, Sail paid off John Silver and went into the nearest hotel.

Sail consulted the lobby clock, appeared surprised that it was only ten-thirty, and lost his haste. He bought Irish pipe tobacco from the girl at the stand.

The girl said, "I'll bet you have trouble buying your clothes."

Sail gave her a stock grin. People didn't say it was a nice day or a bad day. It was, "My God, you're tall!" or, "You're about two men high and half a man wide, aren't you?" or, if it had to be the weather, it was the old one about the weather up there.

He tamped tobacco into a pipe that was as black as his clothing and pulled long, bubbling drags of smoke out of it. A knot of people stood at the end of the lobby and Sail went over to stand, a foot taller than any man in the group, with them. Over their heads, he could see the barometer they were watching.

"It's pumping," a man said, pointing at the barometer.

Sail smoked, consulted the clock from time to time. He was stared at.

When the clock said eleven, he looked up the *Ocean Blue Hotel* in the telephone book. Getting into a pay booth to call the number, he had to stoop.

"Miss Nan Moberly," he said.

The hotel operator rang three times before the receiver came off. Then there was a long pause.

Nan Moberly's voice said, "Yes?" strangely.

Sail put the pipe on the small shelf under the telephone, used the hand which had been holding it to keep sound out of his other ear. He did not speak immediately.

Then he asked, "It go off all right?"

Nan Moberly cleared her throat.

"Sure?"

"Yes." She cleared her throat again, hesitated. "I got to my car.

The doctor I had hired was waiting in it. He brought me to my hotel. Told them I had been hurt. Yes, we put it across all right."

Sail did not speak. He had been straining to get every inflection of her voice.

Nan Moberly said, "Everything is fine."

Sail said, "Somehow you don't sound that way."

The telephone wire was unnaturally quiet for a moment, as if she had put her hand over the mouthpiece. Then she began speaking.

"It's fine. Absolutely fine. Sanders telephoned, and I told him I got to my car while he and Caesar were chasing you. I told him I was not badly hurt. I put Doctor Smith on the telephone—Doctor Smith is the one I hired to help me fake this—and he told Sanders I would pull through. Sanders said he was very sorry I had been robbed, and that he would call on me tomorrow, if Florida was still on the map."

"Then the fake robbery went over, as you wanted?"

"Perfectly."

She was speaking faster than Sail had heard her speak during the four hours he had known her.

He asked, "What about the package?"

"Oh," she said queerly. And it was a full minute before she added, "Where can I have someone pick it up?"

"I can deliver it to you."

"No. Someone might see you. I'll have a boy get it."

Sail made a thoughtful mouth. "I'll be aboard my bugeye, *Sail*, for the next hour. Later, the boat will probably be up the river in a canal somewhere."

"I'll send a boy."

Sail took his hand off his ear, hesitated, put it back again.

He said, "I'd still like to know why you went to all of that trouble. You wanted someone to think you had been robbed. Moreover, you wanted them to think you were too badly injured to leave town."

"Forget it," the girl said tightly. "You've been paid for what you did. Now forget it."

She hung up.

She had not asked whether any of the bullets had hit Sail.

A POLICE TRAFFIC car equipped with a radio was parked in front of the City Yacht Basin. The speaker was bellowing:

"A tropical disturbance is reported to be approaching this section. All boats are advised to seek adequate shelter afforded by the Miami River and adjacent canals. Drawbridges over the river are electrically operated and cannot open if the power supply fails. Please move your boats at once."

Sail made for his boat with long-legged speed.

The bugeye, *Sail,* was a Chesapeake Bay five-log, thirty-four feet waterline. With the look of having been built last week, she was sixty-eight years old. Her beam was twelve feet, she drew two feet with the centerboard up. She was black—hull, stays, sails, sail covers. All black.

Sail swung aboard by the stays, stood looking at the pile of old auto and truck tires on the cabin. There were at least fifteen tires.

John Silver sat on the tires, stuffing a cob pipe. He did not look up until he had struck a match on his wooden leg and set the tobacco afire.

He said, "I like her, Cap'n."

Sail said, "You'll like the dock better."

"Aw, now, mate—"

"Off!"

"Look, now, mate, I put my hack in a nice stone garage until this is over. I haven't anything to occupy myself with, as the saying is. Having seen this sweet ship around here and having seen you aboard her and having seen and heard things—"

"What things?" Sail asked harshly.

John Silver squirmed uneasily. "Gee, mate, don't get the idea I—"

Sail said, "A woman may push me around, but no man—" and started forward.

John Silver scrambled wildly on to the dock.

Sail said, "And take your tires with you!" and began throwing the old auto tires on to the dock.

"You'll need them things for fenders, mate," John Silver said mournfully.

Sail kept on heaving the tires.

The little wooden-legged man said lugubriously, "John Silver has been misunderstood, mate." He hobbled off. His peg-leg had a rubber tip and his departure was surprisingly silent.

Sail slung the last of the tires on the dock, dry-washed his palms and went below. The cabin was neat and contained a great deal of gear cleverly stowed. A sailor's knife with a long blade stood in a leather sheath fastened to the side of a locker where it could be reached from the cockpit. Sail used the knife—it was razor sharp—to cut the cord around the package he had taken from the girl's leather bag.

Long, tightly rolled photographs were inside the package. Six of them. They were not pictures of persons, but of scenery, flat country taken from the air. Approximately in the center of each picture, running the full length of it, was a regular line of rocks. By placing the pictures together, Sail saw he had an area some fifteen miles long by ten wide, the line of white rock forming a perfect ellipse in the center of it.

After he had looked at the pictures for a while, Sail took them into one of the bugeye's two small cabins. Stowage space here was given over almost exclusively to books. He got out a volume of the encyclopedia and looked under, "Geology."

There was a page of pictures showing an oil field from the air. Sail compared the pictures with those from the package. The same sort of stuff, probably, though he was not geologist enough to be sure.

He replaced the pictures in the package and tied it with a string exactly like the one he had cut. He put the packet in his pocket, then turned on the radio in the cabin.

The cover of the motor-box in the cabin served as a table. He lifted it and began getting the small Diesel motor ready to run. The jets needed cleaning. He removed them, got a jet tool and worked with the concentration of a man pulling snake teeth.

The radio warmed up and said, "*—edge of the disturbance now reported passing Bimini, where the wind has attained the velocity of ninety miles an hour. And now we will have a recording of 'There's a Tavern in the Town.'*"

Feet landed on the bugeye cabin top. They landed hard, the way landlubbers somehow always land when they jump on to a boat. The feet shuffled aft, knocking against cleats, fairleads, handrails, and got into the cockpit with a careful slowness that showed the owner either wasn't accustomed to boats or was an old man.

He was about old enough to vote.

HE PEERED AT Sail and said, "You're sure a tall booger."

He had brown eyes and the plumpness of a duck. His shirt and breast pocket handkerchief were ox-blood red. His socks were ox-blood red. The rest of his garments were very white.

He scaled a white envelope down to Sail, not saying anything more. The envelope was unsealed and the enclosure read:

> Please give the bearer the package. Thanks.
> Nan Moberly.

Sail read that.

He said, "Guess I'll have to get my glasses before I can read it."

He put aside the Diesel jet, the jet tool, an S-wrench, then stood. If the cabin headroom had been two feet more, he could have stood straight.

The messenger sounded like a pig squealing as Sail got him by the leg and hauled him down into the cabin.

The plump boy loosened up and fell slackly, the way people fall who know how not to get hurt. He looked startled, frightened, like a puppy that had been kicked. Sail reached for his collar.

The kid got Sail's arm. He got it as a cat gets a mouse.

Sail said, *"Hooo!"* painfully.

White paint in the bugeye cabin was clean and shiny enough to show a shifting, spooky reflection of their fight. No sound they made was louder than the *"in the town… in the town,"* from the radio.

Pain gave Sail's mouth the shape a rubber band takes when it lies loose on a desk. He perspired. He got down on the floor on top of the kid. He breathed through his teeth, sounds like steam escaping.

The plump boy worked on nothing but the arm. He hissed, "How—you—wise—beyond me!" and sounded like a small bulldog with a bone.

Sail finally got two forefingers of his free hand in the boy's nose. He pulled, got the kid's head back. The kid's mouth strained wide open and he sounded as if he were gargling water. Then he came loose. Sail hit him, then got away from him. The boy lay on the black battleship linoleum and trembled.

Sail's right hand, the one the boy had worked on, was out of shape, thumb bent back unnaturally at the second joint.

He shuffled in agony to the companionway and put his head out and looked around. Two men were aloft on the spreaders of a schooner lying at a nearby pier, stripping her of everything—tops'ls, topmasts, halliards, even halliard blocks and chafing gear. Having seen no one around who did not look worried about a boat, Sail backed into the bugeye cabin.

He said, "You tried it alone, eh?"

The plump boy did not answer. He had stopped trembling and was feeling of his jaw where Sail's fist had hit.

Sail gripped his own right hand with his left hand, set himself and jerked hard. He said, "*Sh-h-h-h!*" windily as the thumb went back into joint. Quickly, as if wanting to get it all over with at once, he yanked at the thumb until it looked, if it did not feel, normal.

He sidled around, put a foot on the small of the boy's back, mashed him out flat and searched him. He collected a dog track dope sheet, bet stubs from Hialeah, four dice—two of them loaded—over a hundred dollars in money and a letter which began, *"Sonny Dear:"* and said that Dad was out of a job again and couldn't send any money just now. The letter hoped Sonny Dear would soon make some money, although admitting it was hard for a new osteopath doctor to get started.

"What put you wise, tall stuff?" Sonny Dear snarled.

Sail said, "Nan Moberly didn't sound quite right over the telephone. But I wasn't sure until you cut up."

The plump boy showed his teeth fiercely. "You mean I gave it away?"

"You didn't do anything else." Sail looked at him darkly. "Nan Moberly was scared when she talked to me over the phone. What was wrong there?"

"You slay me, long fellow. Nothing was wrong."

Sail said, "Damned if I'm not going to take time off and find out."

He got a ball of Italian marlin, stripped off an ample length, doubled it several times and lashed the plump boy's wrists and ankles. He used cotton waste and friction tape for a gag. He dipped his fingers in some oil and made the marlin knots too slippery to be untied. His right arm was of little use and the thumb joint was beginning to puff.

He put the plump boy in the oilskin locker, which had air vents, and locked the door.

When he reached the shore end of the dock, John Silver hailed brightly, "Rent a shore cruising craft, Cap'n?"

Sail narrowed his eyes. "Thought your hack was in a stone garage?"

"I got it out, mate."

Sail said suspiciously, "What's the attraction around here, fellow?"

John Silver gulped, "You got me wrong, mate!" and backed away, looking nervous.

Sail stared after him indecisively, shrugged impatiently and lengthened his stride over to another cab, got in, said, *"Ocean Blue Hotel* over at the Beach."

THE STEEL SHUTTERS they were putting on the *Ocean Blue* windows were new and modernistic like the hotel. A desk clerk with a gardenia looked up at Sail and said, "Miss Moberly says you can go right up. Six-O-Nine." An elevator boy said, "Watch your head, Mister." Two men unloading steel storm shutters on the sixth floor corridor stopped work and stared at Sail.

Nan Moberly's voice said, when Sail flipped fingernails against the door of Six-O-Nine, "Come in."

The room was a delicate, lovely red, and all the furniture in it, of metal, was the same hue, except for judicious touches of chromium and a clock embedded in glass that stood on a table by one door, and a modernistic glass ship sailing on the dresser across by the other door.

"Men," Nan Moberly said, "are so darn full of chivalry they make me itch."

She lay on the bed. All of her except her head was under the covers and the covers were tucked in around her neck. There was no one else in the room.

Sail went over and drew up a chair and sat on it beside the bed, about halfway between the foot and head. He did not say anything.

Nan Moberly asked, "What is eating you?"

Sail said, "Imagination."

Nan Moberly tried to swallow twice before she made it. She was keeping a small smile on the corners of her mouth.

"Imagination is exclusively the curse of mankind. The birds and the beasts and the little things that crawl do not have it."

Sail's legs were long and his knees were up high as his feet rested squarely on the floor, and he did not slump as some tall men do, which made him seem taller.

"Want to tell me what you've got yourself into?" he asked.

"What did you mean—imagination?"

Sail said. "The trick you pulled. Faking that robbery. It was so melodramatic it was a laugh. It couldn't work."

"It did work."

"Sure?"

The smile on her lips slipped, but she jerked it back in place. "Of course. Admittedly, it was a bit wild. But I got what I wanted; that package stolen. And I wanted it to appear that I would be laid up for a few weeks."

"The idea being that someone would then lay off you?"

"Maybe."

Sail said, "Sanders and Caesar?"

She was too prompt with her, "No!"

Sail, by looking straight ahead, could gaze across the park, across the beach on which there was one lone bather, and across a dozen miles of ocean to an unnatural looking horizon.

He said, "The name of the doctor you hired to help you out in this was—"

"Doctor Smith," she said shortly. "I told you that."

"Osteopath?"

"No," she said, and looked so puzzled at the question that he knew her answer was truth.

Sail got up and put his left hand on the edge of the bed and aimlessly moved his right hand the small amount it would move without hurting. Nan Moberly returned his gaze for a moment, then fixed her eyes on the ceiling. Her eyes were blue, not actually dull; the effect of dullness was lent by the almost drugged lifelessness of the flesh around her eyes.

Sail said, "You're a geologist, aren't you?"

Her, "Yes," did not move her slightly parted lips.

"I looked at the pictures. That's how I knew. They're pictures of the rocks on the surface of as sweet an oil structure as I've seen in many a day. Why, if there is oil there the pool must be all of fifteen miles long. If I knew more about it, I could talk on and on."

She said barely audibly, "You're doing well enough. But you don't have to broadcast."

Sail said, "At first, I thought it was screwy. But the answer has got to be oil. Air photos frequently locate dome structure favorable to the presence of oil. But they don't guarantee that oil is down there. That's where I'm stumped."

She whispered, "A lake of oil. My company has tapped one end. We don't know which way the lake runs. The pictures show that. They show us where to lease land that will have oil under it."

Sail's, "Hm-m-m," was understanding. "Knowledge that's worth a million—could be several million."

She nodded, went on whispering, "They're the only pictures that have been shot. It takes weeks of work. Before any other company can work the country, we'll have the land bought or leased. That is, if the wrong people don't get my pictures and make me tell exactly where they were taken. I'm the only one who knows that, because the pilot of the plane is dead."

"There's no oil around Miami."

"My boss is en route here from South America. I'm to meet him."

Sail leaned over her. "What's wrong with the setup?"

"Go away," came past her motionless lips in the faintest of whispers. "You can't help now."

Sail took in air, let it out and complained loudly, "It's things like this that women get when they try to wear pants. Women doctors! Women lawyers! Women this and women that! Scheme and connive and finagle, and they think because they don't get hurt that they're good. They don't stop and think that men don't like to push them around. By God, there's too much chivalry in this world!"

In his emphatic earnestness, his fingers clutched the bed cover and dragged it down a bit, as if by accident. The girl's wild look, her cry, "Don't!" would have tipped him off, even if his moving the covers a trifle had been an accident.

He whipped the covers back.

The girl was bound hand and foot with thin white rope.

SAIL PIVOTED, LUNGED to the nearest door and gripped the knob. It was locked and he gave it two hard wrenches, then spun back to the bed. "What's in there?"

"It's another room," she said, very faintly.

"It's a narrow door," Sail said. "So it's a closet door."

Her skin was the color of milk and her lips were an icy blue. Her small teeth, upper and lower, showed, and they were dry and her tongue was also dry. Her eyes began to fill and she blinked, forcing drops out on her lashes. She did not say anything.

Sail looked at the room's third door. His shoulders crawled up in his coat as if something heavy pressed down on the back of his neck, and his hands turned slowly until the palms were forward and the fingers curled slowly, the right ones not as much as the left.

He said violently, "We'll forget the whole thing!" and started for the corridor door, but lifted up silently on his toes, veered over to the room's third door, at the same time fishing a fat blue revolver out of his left trouser pocket.

He broke the gun open while in motion, looked at the cartridges. The cylinder held five shells. Two of them had red paint on their rumps. He set the cylinder so the hammer would fall on a red cartridge, closed the weapon and sat down on the floor.

It was a bathroom door, and there was about an inch of ventilating space between the bottom of the door and the floor. The door opened outward. Sail silently put both feet against it. He shoved the barrel of the gun under the door and pulled the trigger. The report sounded as if he had broken a very old egg.

He sat there, holding the door so it could not be opened. But no one tried to open it. Some of the tear gas he had fired under the door came out of the crack and smarted his eyes. He leaned back, turned his head away from it. He saw under the bed.

Sail straightened up slowly, went to the bed and got one of the covers which he made into a long hank and placed it against the bathroom door, nudging it snugly against the crack with a toe to keep less of the gas from coming out.

He went back, got the dead man by the hand and dragged him out from under the bed.

THE CORPSE HAD gray hair, average height, neat clothing. There seemed to be nothing wrong with him, except that his neck was broken.

Sail said, "Who is it? The doctor you hired to help you fake your story over? Smith—or was that his name?"

Nan Moberly surged up violently on the bed, straining against the white rope until her arms and legs trembled, then fell back.

She gasped, "Get out of here!"

Sail said, "They weren't fooled by your story. They came here to get you. The doctor put up a fight and the osteopath fixed his neck. They made you tell where the pictures were. Now, where are those men?"

She didn't hesitate. "Your boat. They went to see what had happened to the osteopath. He went for the pictures and didn't come back."

"Sure they're not around here? I thought they were in the bathroom, at first."

"I'm sure," she said levelly.

Sail used his sharp pocket knife on the white ropes which tied her, then said, "Go to the *Floridan* and register as—Mary Dallas will do. Stick there until you hear from me or decide you're not going to. O.K.?"

Her "O.K." was with her lips alone.

Sail said loudly, "You know why I'm doing this?"

"No."

"I don't either," he growled.

He swung toward the door.

The closet door which had been locked clicked. It whipped open and fat men tried to get out at once. They stuck. But they had their right arms out and their right hands held guns.

"Alley oop!" they said together.

Sail stopped. His gun was in his trouser pocket, and would probably stick on the cloth, and if it didn't, they could still shoot him before he got his hand in his pocket. He held his arms out straight.

Both fat men had nice suntans, healthy looking skins and good clothing. There was nothing else nice about them.

One said, "Back up, Tom."

"Back yourself. You're the biggest."

They were almost exactly the same size. They got out of the door and Tom said, "You feel him, Doll."

Doll walked over, his hip movement that of a goose, and felt of Sail's clothing. He collected the gun, the pocket knife and the packet of films. Backing way, he began opening the package.

Sail looked at the girl. "Your stock goes up, Nan."

Tom smirked, "She told you that one about us going to your boat to get you clear of the room. She was trying to do you a favor."

Doll said, "But you walking around loose ain't no favor to us."

Then Doll got the package open, held the pictures up to the light and smacked his lips. "This is them, I guess."

Tom looked at Sail and said, "If Sonny Dear was here, it'd make it real simple. He ain't a hell of a good osteopath, but he sure twists a mean neck when somebody knows too much."

THROUGH THE WINDOW Sail could see something coming out in the east, far over the Atlantic Ocean. It was not nice. The sea as far as the eye could see was greasy smooth, but heaving up in great swells which marched up to the beach and climbed the sand for a hundred feet and more, turning into acres of slavering foam.

There was not enough breeze to stir the most fragile palm frond.

Sail said, "Who are you working for?"

"For us," Doll said.

"Probably for Sanders, the guy with the pony legs," Sail corrected.

"Who's Sanders?"

Sail said nothing.

Tom and Doll looked at Nan Moberly. "Who's Sanders?"

The girl wet her lips. "Someone I know."

"He interested in this in any way?" Doll demanded with sudden suspicion.

"No," the girl said.

Tom said heartily, "Now that we've got a man named Sanders all settled, what say we matriculate from this place, as it were."

Knuckles tapped the door twice, gently.

Tom and Doll swapped eye flickers. They put their guns in their pockets and kept their hands in the pockets with them.

Doll called, "Yeah?"

"The storm shutters, Mister," a drawling cracker voice explained. "We're puttin' 'em over the windows."

Doll smirked. "Just a minute until my wife gets her clothes on."

He seized the body of Doctor Smith, hauled it to the closet, dumped it inside and locked the door. Looking around for give-aways, he saw the ropes which had bound the girl. He chucked those out of the window. Then he made his gun and his hand big in his coat pocket.

He told Sail, "They killed Rothstein in a hotel, if you remember back that far. Now, get moving." He moved the pocketed gun.

To the men on the other side of the door, "All right, now."

Two men came in, struggling with a steel shutter. The two men looked too lazy to wipe off their sweat.

One of them peered sleepily at Sail and mumbled cunningly, "Gee whillikers, Mister, do you feel any wind up there yet?"

Doll said, "Hah, Florida humor!" and went out. Sail and Nan Moberly followed, then Tom. The elevator operator who took them down showed no interest in anything but Sail's height.

In the lobby, a man with white whiskers was demanding querulously if the hotel was safe in a hurricane and the other persons there were showing much interest in the desk clerk's reply. Only one small boy stared at Sail. Doll kept close with his gun. Sail didn't pay any particular attention to either Doll or his gun; he went on with a docileness that suggested he was willing to go wherever the two men planned to take them.

Tom and Doll stopped the silent march at a gray sedan. Sail and Nan Moberly sat in the rear. Doll turned down the folding seat and sat on that. Tom turned on the radio and drove.

The radio warmed up and began, *"It is advised that all citizens fill available containers with water to avoid discomfort in case the city water supply should be interrupted. The following hotels have extended an invitation to the public to seek shelter during the disturbance."* Names of the hotels followed.

Doll declared hilariously, "It sounds as if the circus was coming to town."

Sail asked quietly, "Ever attended that special kind of a circus?"

"No."

Sail said, "It'll probably tickle hell out of you."

The car ran silently, and they could hear the sound of hammers at times. At one house, a woman was taking in her lawn furniture. Farther on, they passed a man who was running and who had his head down, as if he had a long way to run.

Doll looked at the girl. "It'd simplify things if you'd cough up now, honey."

The girl said nothing.

Doll shook his head. "We're boys who didn't go to Sunday School, you know."

Nan Moberly said, "What do you take me for? Regardless of where I told you I took the pictures, you would hold me. I think you would torture me just to make sure I had told the truth."

Doll called forward, "What do you know about that, Tom?"

"She reads minds," Tom said.

The car made a corner and Sail swung against Nan Moberly, then straightened himself. He said, "A goofy business, all of it."

Doll shouted to Tom, "Did you hear that? He calls a million or so queer business!"

"Pipe down, fat," Tom advised.

The car pitched them up off the cushions a little as it went over a curbing. The nearest house was at least two hundred yards. Tropical pines grew close to the lane and the car rubbed its gray sides on green needles. Tom put on the brake rather hard.

"Here we be," he said.

THEY WERE CLOSE to Biscayne Bay and a boathouse. A scabby looking boathouse, green around the bottom with moss, more black than white elsewhere. It had been built at least as far back as the big boom.

"Out," Doll ordered.

Nan Moberly quitted the car listlessly and following, Sail tried to look sleepy and resigned.

Tom had a key to the boathouse, but the lock gave him a little trouble and the rusty hinges squealed like a pig stuck in a gate. Two boats were inside. One was a twenty-two foot speedboat which could probably do fifty. The other was a yard or two longer, a job for Gulf Stream fishing—two maple chairs on fixed mountings in the cockpit, a small cabin forward. It might do fifteen knots if pushed.

"In," Doll ordered.

Nan Moberly said swiftly, "If I tell you exactly where I took the pictures, will you let this man go?"

She meant Sail.

"Sure," Doll said.

Sail shook his head at her. "Don't. I'm not sure that you've got what they want. Evidently it's more than the pictures. But you know they killed Doctor Smith, and they won't let you or me go."

Tom came up behind Sail and hit the back of his head with his gun. Sail's knees hinged, his arms hung down, but it did not seem he was going to fall. Then he did, suddenly. He stood very close to the water, on the edge of a concrete slip wall. He started in head first, and Doll leaped and grabbed his legs.

Sail's head and shoulders were in the water. His arms groped, found a projection in the slip wall. One of the board forms had bulged when they poured the wall. He tried to pull himself under the water. Doll pulled to prevent him.

Doll groaned, "Shoot him!"

Tom yelled, "Where?" and leaned over the edge of the slip. Sail gave a jerk, and got into the water, pulling Doll after him. He expected Doll to let go. Doll didn't. Sail swam madly, pulling Doll after him. He came up against the bottom of the fishing boat, and lack of breath began to bother him.

Doll still hung to his ankles. Sail doubled, got hold of Doll. The man felt spongy. He still had his gun. The grip he had on Sail's ankles was a hug. Sail concentrated on getting the gun. It exploded, and for some time thereafter, he heard nothing. But he got the gun.

He came to the surface on the other side of the fishing boat, still fighting with Doll. He got air in his lungs, then clubbed Doll once and Doll relaxed.

Tom came sidling cautiously around the end of the slip. Sail fired at him. It was a good gun, and had not split its cylinder when it went off under water. The bullet broke in one of the boathouse tiles behind Tom and he leaped back.

Sail yelled, "Doll is dead!" for the effect. He hardly heard himself, due to the effects of the shot underwater.

During the next few seconds, he did not hear anything. Then he felt a throbbing in the water and knew the speedboat motor had started. The speedboat was on the other side of the fishing boat and he could not see it.

Doll was senseless, drowning noisily, although Sail still held him. Sail swam quietly, dragging Doll, but the man made enough noise to betray their position. Sail was on the point of abandoning him when the speedboat scooted out of the end of the boathouse open to Biscayne Bay.

Tom, driving the speedboat, and facing back and holding Nan Moberly up in front of him as a shield, fired twice at Sail. The bullets tore splinters out of the fishing craft. Sail did not fire back. The speedboat went toward Miami with no more than its rear third in the water.

Sail hauled Doll out and dragged him, more drowned than not, to the gray sedan and slung him into the front seat.

WHEN SAIL BUMPED the sedan against the curb in front of the City Yacht Basin, there was no other car in the street and no other boat except his black bugeye, *Sail*, at any of the piers. Only one man was visible and he was locking up the lunch stand near Pier Five. Sail got his dripping wet man out of the car. Doll could walk, although he coughed intermittently. As they moved away from the car, a little stream of water ran off the front floorboards and down over the running board to the ground. Their feet sobbed in their shoes, and Sail's hearing had improved enough to get that.

They went out on the dock.

A puff of air hit the left sides of their faces. It died away quickly. There was not a bird in sight. Scooped grapefruit halves, squeezed oranges, paper bags fat with garbage floated on the greasy water.

Something large and black was in the eastern sky.

The bugeye cabin hatch was open. Doll had a spasm of coughing—he was still getting a little water out as Sail pushed him aboard. Sail gave him a chance to climb down into the cabin, but he slipped and fell headlong.

The port cabin kerosene lamp was knocked out of its gimbal mounting and broken. Cushions were off the seat and lay on the floor.

John Silver looked at Sail and made a noise that might have been made by a large, disturbed bumblebee.

He was gagged and roped to the mast, which extended down through the cabin. The knots in the rope had been greased.

Sail removed the gag, but did not untie the ropes.

The peg-leg taxi driver hocked out his mouth, then said, "They greased the knots. Who ever heard of such a thing?"

Sail opened the oilskin locker. Sonny Dear, the osteopath, was not in it. Sail looked in the staterooms, forward in the tiny fo'castle with its one pipe berth and stowed gear, then into a clothes locker, into the head, into a lazaret aft under the cockpit flooring. No osteopath anywhere.

Doll sat on the cabin floor where he had fallen, coughing in long, excruciating spasms, keeping his mouth wide open and taking air in with an "Uh-h-h-h!" between spells. He had skinned his face when he fell down the steps and blood and sweat were mixing on his fat, straining countenance.

John Silver stared at Doll and said, "It was another fat craft like him that moored me to this mast. That one was called Tom."

Sail said, "So now you are going to explain?"

John Silver knocked his wooden leg against the mast as he tried to make himself more comfortable.

"I'm cured, mate," he said. "I want to say that right now. I don't do any more favors. Not for anybody except myself. I'm scuttled, keelhauled and deckwiped if I ever help my fellow-man again."

"Wouldn't it make sense if you told it another way?" Sail demanded impatiently.

"I come down here in the cabin. I hear a noise. It's a man tied up in the oilskin locker. I lay him on the floor and untie his hands. He takes me by the leg and I never seen such a swab. He almost gets me leg. Then he ties me up. How's that, mate?"

Sail said, "Keep it up."

"Look, mate, if you'd untie me—"

"Try talking yourself loose from that mast," Sail suggested.

"Well, break my keel, how was I to know better? He looked like a kid, and I thought I could man a craft like him. How was I to know he could tie reef knots in my arms and legs?"

"What else happened?"

"Well, a fat guy named Tom came in a speedboat. Him and this arm-twisting swab was shipmates. They went away together. I think from their talk there was a girl in the speedboat. And that's the whole story, except that they went south in the speedboat."

Sail said, "Go on. Why did you come aboard in the first place?"

John Silver sighed deeply. "I don't know if you're gonna believe this."

"It's that kind of a story, is it?"

"Look, mate, you love boats, don't you?"

"What has that to do with you?"

"I love boats, too. Every time I see a boat, I have to stop and look at it. I like to get on a boat every chance I get. Take a woman, mate. Every time they see a baby, they want to take it in their arms. It's the same way with me, only it's boats, not babies. It's an instinct, or something."

Sail said nothing. Doll got through his coughing spell and spread out on the cabin floor, weak and perspiring. Sail moved his right hand slowly, feeling the pain that the motion brought from the strained thumb and wrist joints.

John Silver swallowed.

He said, "All the boats had left the yacht basin. This one was still here. I couldn't bear seeing such a sweet craft wrecked. I came aboard to take her up the river myself."

Sail remained silent.

The peg-leg man gulped, "A woman wouldn't leave a little strange baby out in a storm, would she?"

WIND WENT, "*WHOOO-O-O!*" softly in the rigging and the halyards popped against the varnished masts and the boat leaned over slightly. The puff died quickly, and the bugeye straightened and sat calmly in the little waves that fluttered against the hull planks.

Unseen hooks seemed to take hold of the corners of Sail's mouth and pull them back until the lips were taut, blue. He looked at the peg-leg and strained his weathered hair with his fingers.

Then he swung back suddenly and put his foot on Doll, held him down and began tying him. He finished off the rope ends with a crabber's eye knot which was harder to untie than a bowline.

Sail got a slim red bottle of tabasco sauce out of the refrigerator and unscrewed the top. He leaned down quickly and shook a drop of the stuff in the fat man's mouth, and the fellow jumped as if it were a globule of molten lead.

Doll spat, blew over his burning tongue and made a face.

Sail said, "You ever have this stuff in your eyes?"

Doll's eyes popped and parts of his torso bulged as he strained at the ropes. The skinned place on his face began to run red again.

"Hell, Jack!" he gurgled. "Have a heart!"

"I've got a heart, fat man. That's why I'm going to put your eyes out if you don't come across with where they took that girl. I like that girl. She does cuckoo things, and I wouldn't want her around as a fixture, because she'd probably get me killed in no time. But I like her, even if she is funny. And I'm going to bat for her. Where is she?"

Sail spoke slowly and his voice was no less earnest because he did not lift it. Then he pried open one of the fat man's eyes.

Horror opened Doll's mouth wide. He started to pump out a scream. Sail, grabbing a fistful of the fat lips, held most of the sound back. Sail twisted the lips cruelly, ground them against the teeth, pounded the man's head on the floor.

"Where," he gritted, "is she?"

"Angelfish," Doll croaked.

Peg-leg John Silver added, "On a cabin cruiser named the *Oilman.*"

Sail came around, grabbed the peg-leg man's shoulders. "How'd *you* know?"

"Heard Tom tell the arm-twisting kid as they got in the speedboat," John Silver said calmly. "They said something about it being twenty-five or thirty miles away."

"That sounds like Angelfish," Sail said.

"What is Angelfish, mate?"

"Angelfish Creek. It's a tide gut between two mangrove keys south of here."

Wind came again outside. It said, *"Wheee-e-e!"* this time, and the bugeye heeled more. An empty box someone had forgotten on the dock turned over and over with a quick procession of thumps like something running.

Sail said hoarsely, "Angelfish! My God!"

HE LURCHED, TALL and strained looking, to the companion and put his head out. The wind took hold of locks of his hair and shook them a little. The sky looked unnatural, full of brassy threat. The halyards were bowed out and the owner's flag and club burgee were trembling at the tips of the masts.

Drops of perspiration came out on Sail's forehead and were pushed around by the wind. He slammed back into the cabin, took Doll by the throat.

"You sure about Angelfish?" he gritted savagely.

Doll looked at the tall weathered man in black and plainly couldn't understand why he was so worked up.

"Yeah. Angelfish it is."

Sail asked, "What kind of a boat?"

"It's got a motor in it, and a lot of room. It ain't cramped like one of these damn sailboats. It's a swell boat. It's a power boat. They'll be all right."

Sail released him and stepped back. He said, "A power boat! A gaudy, unballasted, topheavy crate with two-inch ribs and three-quarter inch planking." He stopped and breathed deeply. "Swell for what they're intended for! Sundays on the Sound or the Bay, or day trips outside."

Doll mumbled, "A little wind. What the hell?"

Sail shook his head slowly. "You're the guy who never saw old man *whee!* doing his stuff. It's too bad you never went down to Matecumbe Key to see the railroad rails tied in knots half a mile back in the mangroves, or the tug that was put three-quarters of a mile inshore on Knights Key."

Outside, the wind suddenly stopped, went absolutely dead. The bugeye jumped up and down on little waves. The springlines strained and the halyards slatted.

John Silver asked, "You're trying to make up your mind, ain't you?"

Sail said, "I was waiting for a lull so we can get out of this slip," and bounded out into the cockpit. The Diesel, starter and all, was controlled from there. He got it banging over, leaped forward, flung off the bow springlines, came aft, cleared the stern springlines from the bitts that were like little square posts.

He was about to put the clutch in gear when he seemed to make up his mind about something. He left the wheel, let the bugeye bob out toward the middle of the slip, and came long-armed and long-legged down into the cabin.

He got the sailor's knife out of the sheath beside the companion in passing. He slashed peg-leg John Silver loose from the mast.

"On the dock with you," Sail said. "You're not going."

"Huh? Listen, mate—"

"You fool," Sail said. "Anybody who has been through one of these things respects them from that time on."

"It ain't that."

"Then what is it?"

"I'm a company dick," John Silver said.

"A what?"

"A private detective employed by the oil company which also

employs Nan Moberly," John Silver elaborated. "I was sent here to watch Nan Moberly."

THE BUGEYE RAN out of the slip between the City Yacht Basin piers, clearing the dolphins about equidistant, riding her clipper bow high like a graceful black swan. Sail put the wheel over, headed her south toward the row of finger-boards that marked the dredged channel down toward Cape Florida. He screwed down the clamp that lashed the wheel, then galloped forward, unstopped the stays'l and yanked it up. He did the same with the fores'l.

He started to lift the main, looked back and saw that another puff of wind was coming. Leaping to the cockpit, he paid out the sheets that led back to cleats around the cockpit.

The puff hit. The water got varicose veins all around them. The bugeye seemed to lift itself a foot and rush forward.

John Silver said, "Hully-gee! We got wings!"

The first dredged channel marker went past with a sucking sound. The wind was almost astern now. It got in Sail's hair and stretched it out ahead. Every little wave around them was breaking.

Sail yelled, "Get below and make everything fast!"

John Silver went below, agile on his wooden leg.

Sail reached forward and jerked the canvas cover off the compass binnacle, wadded it, and hurled it down the companion. The first of the tall, channel range lights went past. The channel dog-legged a little there, and he made the turn.

Spray, picked up by the wind, came aboard, beating his back, smashing against the little dinghy, which was lashed to the stern davits, bugeye fashion.

Then the wind died again. That was the way with some hurricanes when they began. Gusty.

The bugeye lost headway until the push of the Diesel picked up. Sail lashed the wheel again and went to the companionway.

Voices were below.

John Silver was saying, "—and you ain't kidding me any, fat boy! Sancaese and Company hired you boys to get those films from Nan Moberly. Sancaese and Company, the cheapest scabs in the oil business. They haven't any money to spend on honest surveys of their own. So they watch my company. They see our engineers surveying in New Mexico. If the pictures from the plane show oil dome formation, we will naturally lease a few sections and sink a well. If Sancaese and Company can find out what the pictures show, they can step in and lease the ground ahead us." The peg-leg man stopped to snort. "They don't want to drill themselves. Oh, no! They just want to resell the leases to us at a big profit!"

Doll said wearily, "Oh, hell! Do you have to stand there and gobble at me?"

"I'll do more than gobble if Nan Moberly gets hurt!" John Silver yelled. "Damn my company! They thought she might sell out to Sancaese. So they send me to watch her. And I watch her and things begin to happen and before long, damned if I ain't a wooden-legged man who is well mixed up. Now, you're gonna tell me—"

Sail called, "Are you making things fast down there?"

John Silver was silent for a while, then said, "O.K."

Sail went back to the wheel, for the wind had come again more slowly than before, which was a bad sign. The bugeye surged and began to run like a mad blackbird.

The peg-legged man came on deck, holding on to things. "How long'll it take us?"

"Depends on the wind. There'll probably be too much or too little."

"Is this the hurricane?"

The wind made the noises of three or four violins in the rigging.

"That," Sail said, "is just the little pups that hang around the skirts of the mother wolf."

THE WAVES CAME up around them, the short, steep waves that make shoal water so deadly. Biscayne Bay, for all its several miles of width and its more than a score miles of length, was nowhere much more than two fathoms deep.

This time, the wind blew steadily, with increasing force. The waves white-capped, then began to come to pieces on top.

Spray lifted up in hissing, twisting sheets and came aboard. The scuppers got brimful and the cockpit sloshed ankle deep, the self-bailing pipes unable to keep up. The bugeye rolled, pitched, bounced, knocked up clouds of spray which the wind caught and rushed on ahead. And the sky above was turning leaden.

John Silver got back beside Sail and clung to the cockpit rail. He opened his mouth to say something. The wind got in past his teeth and made him cough. He faced the other way, got his mouth close to Sail's ears. Then he yelled:

"You probably think pictures and what they mean is a hell of a thing to fight over, mate. If it was money, that'd make sense. But you gotta know the oil business, the way they work it the modern way, and then it makes sense."

Sail roared back, "Get ropes for us to lash ourselves."

"O.K. But I thought—"

Sail bellowed, "It makes sense. I've heard that these airplane survey pictures are sent around the oil fields under armed guard, to keep rival outfits from copping them."

John Silver nodded, lurched up to get the ropes. The bugeye yawed, rolled rail under, sank dizzily in a wave trough and the peg-leg man went skidding for the Bay. Sail got him, kept him aboard, and fought the boat back on its course.

John Silver yelled, "I ain't so spry. You get the ropes. I'll steer, mate."

Sail said, "You never steered a boat in your life."

The peg-leg man looked disappointed. "How'd you know, mate?"

"No sailor," Sail said, "ever talked quite like you do."

John Silver grinned, put his face close to Sail's and howled, "I was practicin' up on foolin' people. I'm just an oilfield tool pusher who turned half-pants dick after he neglected to keep his leg out of a bullwheel."

He got the ropes, after some difficulty. They tied themselves to cleats, allowing about six feet of play in the line.

The cockpit got level full of water and the weight helped keep the stern of the bugeye down. Waves came up behind and bumped the dinghy on the stern davits and before long the davits began to bend. Finally, the flat bottom came out of the dink, except for a few fragments.

Once, when it lulled a little, though, they did hear Doll below in the cabin. He sounded like a bleating sheep.

Two shoal banks crossed the lower end of Biscayne Bay, Sail knew. The first had a wide opening, with markers. When he saw how high the water had risen on them. Sail didn't worry as much about the next bank, which was Arsenicker, and bad.

But the next bank, the last one they had to cross, was wide, and it was breaking water for half a mile. The fores'l blew out in that. One moment it was pulling, the next it was a trembling canvas beard along the spars.

Rain caught up with them. Sheets of it traveling along above the water, seeming never to fall, moving so fast that the eye had difficulty following it. Flag and burgee had turned to strings on the mast tips. And the American Jack on the stern staff had narrowed down until it was not much wider than a hand.

They kept their hands over their mouths so they wouldn't breathe water and Sail angled in toward Angelfish.

THE CABIN CRUISER was a forty-two footer, all white and mahogany, and a sweet thing to tie up to a swanky club dock. There was a lot of glass windows around her cabin, and two neat little varnished lapstrake dinghies were davited, one on each side.

The glass had all been blown out of her cabin. One dink was gone. The other had come loose from the stern davit, had swung over, and was slamming up and down, patting a hole in the cabin top.

There seemed to be about two feet of water inside her.

She had anchored in a mangrove creek, but the wind had pushed her out and she was drifting down on the mangroves on the other side. The *Sail* came in ahead of her. She would never come up into the wind under stays'l alone.

There was no sign of life aboard her.

Sail left the wheel, raced forward, used his sheath knife on the lashings of the heavy anchor. Three hundred pounds of iron, it was. Ridiculously large for such a small boat. And the chain was heavy in proportion.

Sail let it go. The chain ran over the winch wildcat and was arranged so it couldn't jump out. The winch had a brake. Sail came down on it.

The anchor took hold; its yank ducked the whole front of the boat. Sail reached out with the knife and stuck the stays'l. The sail went to pieces with a noise like cats fighting.

The hooker was the *Oilman*. And the *Sail* was hanging directly ahead of her by no more than a hundred feet.

Sail got down on all fours and hung onto things and got back to the wheel. He set it to port, locked it. The bugeye swung over, for water was rushing past underneath just as air was rushing on top.

He went forward and let out chain until he had the bugeye back even with the cruiser. Then he half-hitched the chain over the winch bollards.

A boil of water came over the bugeye four or five feet deep and left John Silver hanging at the end of his lashing line. Sail hauled him back, put his mouth against the peg-leg's ear.

"I'll swing her in and board," he shouted. "You swing her off, then bring her back again when and if I clean house."

Sail jockeyed the wheel, and the stream of water moving past and pressing against the rudder caused the bugeye to swing on her chain in toward the power boat. He was facing the wind now. His polo shirt and trouser hugged one side of his body and ballooned out on the other. And he could see at all only when he held his open hand over his eyes and squinted between the fingers.

Sail gave John Silver the wheel. He pulled himself amidships. The bugeye shouldered against the cruiser. Sail was pitched aboard. He got in the deckhouse.

John Silver sheered the bugeye off.

The osteopath came clawing up out of the cruiser's forward cabin and Sail kicked him in the face.

Sail thought of the doctor with the broken neck, and of his own arm which still hurt, and he kicked hard, permanently altering the fat young man's dentistry and driving him back to land in a water-filled cabin and splash water over the walls.

Sail followed him down, getting his gun out. Caesar, the very fat, very blond Viking, had been bucketing water out through a porthole.

He dropped his bucket, squawled, "Yumpin' Yoseph!" and dug at his big bright guns harnessed under his arms.

Sail shot tear gas in his eyes. Caesar went backward as if it had been lead, then began to shoot both his guns aimlessly.

The boat rolled. Mattresses, folding chairs, canned goods, and the osteopath sloshed around on the floor. Sail, looking swiftly, saw no sign of Nan Moberly. The gas got to his eyes and he retreated, made it up the companionway. He fell down in the deckhouse. What was left of the windows was washing over the floor. He cut himself on that. Caesar's guns still spoke below.

The boat, being built for complete privacy, had no means of entrance from the deckhouse into the rear cabin. It was necessary to go outside and fight along the rail, dodging the swatting efforts of what was left of the lapstrake dink.

He reached the rear companion slide and jacked it open. He put his mouth close to the slide, but not close enough that his face could be seen from within the cabin, and screeched, "Hey! Help!"

Tom, the other fat man, put his head out and Sail was ready, although he never did know for sure but that he hit too hard. He wasn't trying to kill anybody, particularly.

He dived down after Tom.

There was a port bunk and a starboard bunk. Sanders, the man with the draft horse legs, lay on one bunk. His face was a tint of green and he had messed up the bed and the jacket life preserver he was wearing.

Nan Moberly lay bound in the other bunk.

The cruiser jumped up on a wave and shook itself. Tom's slack body got between Sail's feet and he fell down. Sanders, suddenly losing his seasickness, came off his bed and began to stamp and kick Sail.

Sail lost his gun. He rolled to get away from Sanders' powerful kicking. Landing on his back, he drew back his long legs and kicked once himself. Sanders took it where he probably felt the worst. His stomach. He staggered back against the companion.

The kick took it out of him. Evidently he didn't have a gun. He wheeled, scrambled up the companion. Sail lurched after him and got one of Sanders' legs. They had a fight over the leg and Sanders won.

Sail clawed out on deck after Sanders. The man looked back, saw him, and tried to make more speed. He took a chance, not holding onto the handrail.

The first lurch of the boat put him overboard, and the tide rushed him away, riding high in his life preserver.

SAIL BACKED INTO the cabin, floundered to the girl and was pitched into the bunk with her by the motion of the boat. He cut her ropes. She could move, and they reached the deck. Sail waved.

He waved three times before John Silver saw them, and sheered the bugeye over and caved in half the side of the power boat. Sail and Nan Moberly landed to the bugeye deck.

The bugeye bounced away, a wave curled over it, broke in froth and violence. When Sail looked, the military mast of the cruiser was just pulling itself beneath the surface.

He tumbled into the cabin with the girl, got up, thrust his head out of the companionway, looked, and after a while saw Sanders. The man had been washed into the tops of the mangroves. He had left his life jacket hanging on one of the snags, but was clinging to the other, high enough so that only the tallest waves tossed him about.

Sail saw no sign of the men who had been in the cruiser a little while ago.

He yelled, "Come below!" at John Silver.

The peg-legged fellow tumbled into the cabin. Sail shut the hatch.

He turned on the radio.

Doll, still sick, moaned loudly.

Sail looked at Nan Moberly, at the company detective with the wooden leg. He saw what they were thinking.

"Sanders," Sail said. "He's back in the mangroves. We can't help him. Maybe he'll tough it out."

John Silver peered at Nan Moberly. "What was the line-up, Nan?"

"Those pictures show an oil formation," the girl said dully.

"And only I know where they were taken. Sancaese and Company—Sanders and Caesar—tried to buy the location from me. I refused. They said they'd get it anyway. I hired Mister Sail, here, to—"

Sail said, "Explain that later. The thing you can tell me now is why you bore those two punks out when they told me Sanders and Caesar were not it."

Nan Moberly said, "As long as you didn't know the truth, I thought they might let you off."

The radio, cracking and popping, said: *"It is now evident that only the edge of the tropical disturbance is going to touch the Florida coast. Reports from Fowey Rocks and elsewhere indicate...."*

John Silver gulped, "Hully-gee—ain't this thing we been having *it?*"

"Only the pups," Sail said.

He muttered, "We should try to drift a life preserver to Sanders on a long line," and put his head out of the hatch.

Successions of brown muddy waves were curling over the mangroves, breaking with sudsy turbulence, smashing one after another upon Sanders, and finally the water tore him loose and bore him away. He stayed on top for a while, his head back, his mouth wide open.

He was talking to his mother and his God in a loud screaming voice.

Nan put one ear against Sail's chest and clapped a hand over the other. It kept out that sound.

Jungle Impulse

SHE WAS A fair, lean-limbed woman who swam through the dark water in her naked skin. Her hair was long and braided in a pigtail and the end of the pigtail was tied with a string, so the hair did not hamper her swimming.

The night was still, black and warm, and the water was warm. The woman swam in almost complete silence, now that she had managed to stop her sobbing.

A moment ago, when she had seen the flatboat drift around the river bend, she had cried a little from delight.

It had seemed like years—it was eleven days, she believed—since her plane had come down in the river and sank. Stark terror had taught her that they had told her the truth about this jungle. During those eleven days she had suffered in the stupefying heat where bellbirds and noisy toucans planed; she had crouched behind the buttress-like roots of *ceibas,* sharing her hiding places with black thumbless spider monkeys which skulked and trembled like old men. And frequently—she'd come to always expect the sound again soon—the death screech of some poor creature, a sound that made each one of her nerves shake. The death screeches were the soul of the jungle as she had come to know it.

Of late, whenever she remembered the radiantly confident smiles she'd given the newsreel cameras, an hysterical giggling started and wouldn't stop. This frightened her, for she was Nelia Belden, and the world well knew that she was supposed to have no fear.

She was Nelia Belden. Which was supposed to make her pretty extraordinary. She had done so much that sometimes she felt old at twenty-two—people generally believed she was older than that, yet she looked younger. She was a stunningly pretty girl, just a little regal. Most men were scared of her, the average male preferring to wear the chest hair in his family. After an average male heard about the time the Tugeri headhunters besieged Nelia Belden for six days, he was apt to crawl away.

It had been profitable. It had been a calculated and planned business. The idea had occurred to her after she got what she considered a lucky break, and became leading debutante of the season. They called it No. 1 Glamor Girl now. Ordinarily it lasted for a few weeks; maybe it lasted longer if you were good newspaper copy and good camera fodder.

She had made herself a job. The job was the nation's adventure girl. She was not American First Family; she wasn't even Park Avenue. She was only a tall, daring girl whose folks had come from Oklahoma with some oil money, most of which they'd lost. It was a good background.

The exploring racket was slipping; it was a dying horse. But Nelia Belden jumped on; she was good copy and good camera fodder, so she made the old nag gallop. She flew to Australia, via the South Sea Islands, and got stranded on an uninhabited island. She had no food. She ate plankton. What are plankton? They're the little sea organisms on which whales live. Depend on Nelia Belden to come up with the unusual.

Two weeks ago, she'd been making a publicity flight around South America in a new type of light plane. She was getting paid for it. Arthur Bottorff, a fat man who was as nervous as a rabbit, offered her much extra money to make aerial photographs of this stretch of jungle.

Arthur Bottorff explained that he was with the Magellan and Amazon Oil Corporation, which wanted an aerial photographic map of the section. No other plane was available, he explained nervously. Since she had plenty of time, Nelia saw no reason why she shouldn't take him up.... It was the second day when, inexplicably, gasoline started pouring from the tank, and she landed on the river and her plane immediately sank.

And now, a few minutes ago, she had cried from delight when a boat appeared around a bend in the river.

The boat was ugly and flat-bottomed and encircled by a barricade of corrugated sheet iron to keep out arrows. Arrows tipped with a goo made from the climbing *strychnos toxifera* and the poison fangs of snakes and black and red ants.

She swam close to the boat.

"Hello there," she called. "How about taking on a passenger?"

On the boat, Tom Sail jumped slightly—he had iron nerves—and Nickie Sorenson, who was guarding the stern, went up a yard and his cocked rifle let go an accidental ear-splitting crack.

"What was that?" gasped Sorenson.

"It sounds as if we've found Nelia Belden," Tom Sail said.

Later Nelia remembered that he sounded distressed about it even then.

Tom Sail poked a flashlight over the side of the boat, then hastily extinguished the light and swore.

"Run and grab a pair of my pants," he told Sorenson.

Nelia put on the pants in the water and they were so long that they encased her almost completely. She had tied her clothing in a bundle on her head when she started to swim, then lost it—but she didn't explain this, because she was wondering what kind of a giant could own such pants.

"Coming aboard." Tom Sail leaned down and extended to her a hand that felt like a warm rock when she grasped it. She was pulled aboard.

He wasn't as terribly big as she had expected. Still, he was a man obviously made of jaw and fists. His size and his brownness fascinated her immediately.

"I hope rescuing me won't be a trouble," she said.

"It will," said Tom Sail gruffly, and he walked away.

The answer slapped Nelia. She took hold of her lower lip with her teeth and was glad her face was wet anyway, because tears wouldn't show. Ordinarily she was no crybaby, but just now her stamina had hit low ebb.

Afterward, when she got hot coffee and some solid food inside her, she was bothered about it.

"He wasn't exactly civil," she told Nickie Sorenson. "What was wrong?"

Nickie Sorenson wore a queer expression for a moment.

"I wouldn't let it throw me," he said—evasively, Nelia thought.

Nickie Sorenson was a dark young man with thick hands and thick ears. He was solemn; he reminded Nelia of a brown tombstone. Practically any time she glanced at him, he was sure to be watching her.

"Don't mind me," he apologized. "I've got a wife and two kids, and I'm faithful to all three. But I like to look at nice things."

"What do you do?"

"Us? We're explorers."

"I am sort of a flying explorer myself," Nelia explained. "I was taking pictures, and I had some bad luck."

"We already know," said Nickie Sorenson. "We've got a radio."

Tom Sail—he made a long tower of darkness—was standing moodily in the bow with a flashlight as long as his arm and a rifle. Nelia pointed at him.

"What's the matter with him?" she asked.

"I don't believe I would ask him."

Nelia was puzzled.

She slept on a pallet on the deck. At least, she tried. Most of the rest of the night, she twisted and turned fitfully. Now that she was safely rescued, she was having difficulty keeping hold of her nerves.

WHEN MORNING CAME, the river spread much wider, the boat nosed toward shore and Nelia surmised they were drawing near camp. All around and flung away to the sky was the jungle, vivid green, and the sky was pale brass.

Tom Sail stood in the bow. If he had moved since the night before, it was not apparent. Nelia approached him.

"I guess we're coming close to camp," she said.

"Yes."

"I understand you're explorers."

"Yes."

"Any particular kind of exploring you do?"

"Oil."

She could kick him on the shins, or she could walk away. Either course would have been justified. Instead, she stood there and noticed how his copper-brown eyes crinkled at the corners. She sighed.

"When will I be able to leave?" she asked.

Tom Sail frowned quickly, then looked off into the distance.

"We don't have a radio transmitter," he said with something that she didn't understand in his voice. "You can't leave until our supply plane flies in, I guess. A month from now, maybe."

"A month!" Nelia gasped.

The camp was far short of comfortable. It stood back from the river, in a natural clearing; in such a small clearing, Nelia decided a plane couldn't possibly land there—later she saw wheel prints where one had.

There were five men besides Tom Sail and Nickie Sorenson. They lived in round thatched huts called *anthitls*. Inside these huts was coarse jungle grass for floors, and the kind of furnishings you could lock up in a tin duffle box, or that the ants could not eat. They made Nelia welcome; Tom Sail gave her his *anthitl*.

But there were two or three things wrong.

First, there was always a guard posted. Usually he was in the very top of a high tree, with binoculars; he watched the sky rather more than the jungle.

Nickie Sorenson noticed Nelia's curiosity.

"Indians," he explained. "Real ones. No fooling."

Second, the thatched huts, the *anthitls*, were not built in the clearing, but close to the jungle, under overhanging trees, which could have been to make more room for a plane to land in the clearing.... It could have.

There was nothing phony about the portable—portable by airplane—core-drilling rig that stood like a steel mosquito with its beak buried in the jungle, boring for a taste of black blood down below somewhere. But the rig was not tall enough to project above the trees.

Nelia discovered that the crew were nice fellows who weren't going to tell her anything.

They swore by Tom Sail, she also found. They were talking one night around the campfire, and she listened.

"Most men think the money you get makes a job; I know better than that, it's who you work for," one of them said earnestly.

"With me," Nickie Sorenson remarked, "Tom Sail swings more weight than a ton of steel. He always will."

Nelia learned a lot listening to them.

Nickie Sorenson had known Tom Sail for a long time. They had learned geology together, and they had done a lot of other things together, things that make men feel deep friendship. Two of the other men had joined them later, up in Alaska, where they were taking low-grade quartz from a vein that petered out and left them all stranded. They ran geology for oil in California, on the flats around Bakersfield. They drifted into seismographing, at which they made money, because Tom Sail had driving force and was a natural leader, ably backed up by uncanny ability at computing a seismograph recording.

Nelia gathered a world of information from what they said that evening. She found that Tom Sail was a man's man, liked by men, and that he owned his own company, which was camped right here in this clearing, every man-jack of it.

She did not find out why he was avoiding her.

Because she found him an interesting man—she made no attempt to deny to herself that this was so—it disturbed her. She puzzled about it, but did not try to talk about it to him.

However, from the very beginning she found herself liking

the life. The men all wore chainmail shirts of light alloy metal for protection against arrows. They gave her one. She went out with them, watched them do seismographing with genuine interest.

NELIA STOOD ONE night in the darkness at the river's edge, near where the boat was tied. She had been standing there some time.

It was an extraordinarily melting night, a slight breeze bearing the perfume of tropical flowers; up beyond the lacy design of the jungle foliage the stars were as jewel dust. Nelia had been thinking: What a swell world!

Tom Sail touched her arm. "You would be safer in your tent," he said.

She didn't think she was in any danger. Furthermore, she wondered if that was why he'd hunted her up.

"I like your work," she told him. "I might learn it."

Apparently the night had worked a spell on him.

"New and wonderful stuff, seismographing." He launched out with the voluble enthusiasm of a successful man for his work. "In its simplest form, it is this: You bounce sound waves off the entrails of the earth and thereby learn about those entrails. You pole a twelve-pound shot of sixty per cent dynamite down a hole three hundred feet deep, then plant thirty-six geophone jugs and wire them to the black-light-tight recording tent. You fire the hot stuff with two caps. After that, if you're lucky, you have a piece of film bearing some intricate zig-zag lines. It someone walked, or an animal moved in the jungle, you do it over again. Three to nine repeats is an average."

"You mean like a motion picture director shooting his scenes over and over for perfection?"

"That's it. In the end you have a film which a computer can examine and tell all about the anticlines, the monoclines and the domes. That is the modern way of finding oil."

"Dangerous, isn't it?"

"Here in the jungle, you mean?" His slow grin showed that he liked the danger. "It has its moments," he admitted.

By now, Nelia knew a secret about herself. Commencing each time her eyes ranged Tom Sail's corded height and masculine face, something irresistible was happening to her. She was glad.

"Tom," she said suddenly, "why do you dislike me?"

Instantly he had made a bower for her with his long arms, and she was inside it. He kissed her. And breathlessly, "I love you," he said in a voice that quivered. "Do you love me?" he asked.

"If I don't," she murmured, "I'm the victim of some new and wonderful tropical fever."

He kissed her again. Their faces were close together, very bright in the moonlight.

"Darned if you haven't been taking a queer way of showing how you felt," Nelia said.

Her words seemed to snap on an ugly light. Immediately she felt his withdrawal from her; his warmth became frozen, and he retreated back into his previous shell of restraint.

"Nothing is wrong," he said tonelessly. "Nothing." Then he blurted something about seeing after the watchman, and left her.

Nelia gave the boat an angry kick.

"I'll be damned," she said miserably.

It did not help her state of mind to see that he was suffering.

He seemed to be fighting with himself; while the battle was going on, he painstakingly avoided her. He rushed off alone into the jungle before sunrise, before the others were up, to range the tangled labyrinth alone. Or he skulked in his tent, pretending to study the films which bore the seismograph recordings.

It went along like that for two days.

THE SECOND NIGHT was a hot one and Nelia slept fitfully. But it would have made no difference how soundly she slumbered, for when Nickie Sorenson screamed, it was a noise fit to wake the dead. Nelia ran toward the sound.

"What is it?" she gasped.

Tom Sail went right on with what he was doing, which was using wire-cutters to snip off one end of an arrow close to Nickie Sorenson's chest. Then he pulled the arrow out.

"This arrow isn't poisoned," Tom Sail said.

"Food for thought there," Nickie Sorenson suggested weakly.

Tom Sail stood there, thoughtfully turning the arrow in his hands.

"Do I bubble when I breathe?" Nickie asked.

"No."

"Then I don't need a hospital. I can stay here in camp."

Tom Sail finally nodded, but his face was all knotted up with worry.

"If the arrow wasn't poisoned," Nelia said, "it wasn't Indians."

"That's what we're thinking about," he muttered.

No one slept the rest of that night, but nothing else happened.

The next afternoon, the camp had visitors. They said they were platinum prospectors who had banded together for protection from the natives while they were en route to the mountains. They were seventeen of them. Each man had a new rifle. They were shepherded by a man who said his name was Fierst.

Fierst lost no time in casting an appreciative eye upon Nelia. Just one eye—they were very crossed, and only functioned one at a time. His beamy arms hung straight down at his sides, and he was a man who might have been made of lignum vitae, one of the toughest woods known.

Personally, Nelia thought she had never seen a more bedraggled looking outfit than the visitors. She did not see anything wrong with them. When she saw how white Tom Sail had become, it startled her.

Tom Sail whispered to one of his men, who picked up a box that Nelia happened to know contained canned tomatoes. The man carried the box to the center of the camp.

"We've found platinum here," he announced loudly. "Come and look at it."

The trick worked and the visitors gathered around.

Tom Sail capped and short-fused a stick of sixty per cent dynamite and lighted a cigarette. He tucked a case of dynamite under his other arm and walked over to the visitors.

Tom Sail's men broke and ran. Tom Sail himself gave the strangers a short speech, holding the lighted cigarette half an inch from the fuse.

"You've got less time than nothing," he said, "to drop your guns." They had no trouble understanding him, because he said it in a voice that frightened the parrots miles away.

The visitors knew all about Tom Sail, Nelia realized. They showed it by the way they acted. They didn't doubt for a minute that he meant what he said. Neither did Nelia. She experienced such fright that she seemed to stop living.

"Come pick up their rifles," Tom Sail called to his own men, and they came out of the jungle. They gathered the rifles. They herded the prisoners together. The captives were terrified, with the exception of Fierst.

Fierst stood with his long arms hanging at his sides, certainly not scared, and nothing sheepish about his manner except the little down-twist at the ends of his mouth. He was a South American, Nelia decided, although his English had been spoken with no accent. And a brave man.

"You've damned good reason to be scared. You put an arrow into one of my men," Tom Sail told them.

"That's ridiculous," the cross-eyed Fierst disclaimed mildly, hardly trying to make it convincing.

"Don't lie. The arrow wasn't the native kind, and it was not poisoned. Few white men know how to mix the poison, which probably explains why you didn't use it." Sail's tone was lashing and his eyes were like molten copper. He jammed his hands in his pockets and stood there for a while. Finally he gave a pebble a savage kick, "We're going to turn you loose. So start running."

A disappointed howl came from his own crew. He turned on them, "We can't keep this many prisoners; we can't massacre them either, like they probably would have done to us," he pointed out.

The dirty men ran into the jungle, followed by Fierst, who traveled at a lope, frequently looking back over his shoulder.

"Follow them," Tom Sail told one of his men. "For God's sake, don't let them catch you."

AFTER THE CAMP was peaceful again, Tom Sail whirled

and came to Nelia. He came purposefully. When he had confronted her, Nelia saw that there was more suffering than ever on his tanned face.

"After this," he said gravely, "you will stay in camp. Do not leave it."

"I don't understand all this."

"Of course you don't."

Nelia stared after his expanse of shoulders. The depth of his emotion had stunned her. Or his splendid courage. She wasn't sure which.

She did understand that he had just saved all their lives with one almost insanely brave gesture. She realized that the man Fierst and his followers had entered the camp for the exact purpose that Tom Sail believed. There was nothing much else about the situation that she understood.

The man Tom Sail had sent out to scout came back. "They had spare guns hidden," he reported. "They've got them."

"That makes a nice prospect," Tom Sail said.

Nelia entered her thatched hut and stretched out on the cot, the legs of which stood in tin can lids which contained kerosene to discourage climbing insects. She remained there, thinking, until darkness came. By that time, she knew she must confront Tom Sail and have it out with him. He must tell her what stood between them.

Stepping outside, she caught sight of Tom Sail moving out of the firelight toward the jungle. She moved so that she was not noticed and followed Tom.

Some distance into the jungle, she caught up with him. He was crouched over some object, shielding the glow of a flashlight with one hand.

She saw what he was doing. Working a small radio transmitter.

He had told her they had no radio transmitter. She blurted it out. "You said there was no transmitter."

He sprang up. "I told you to stay in camp."

A hurt resentment welled inside Nelia. Her hands tightened into such knots that they ached.

"You lied to me!" she accused.

His answer was slow coming. "Yes, I've lied to you," he said hollowly. "I guess I've lied from the first. Now go back to camp and forget about it."

"What are you doing now?"

"I'm radioing for a plane to take you out of here. Something that even a fool would have done a week ago."

Nelia left him there and walked back to camp. The encounter had shaken her, and she did not know what to do.

None of the men were sleeping this night, she saw. They had their rifles, and they had dug small pits in the ground for themselves, away from the firelight.

"You and I are supposed to sleep on the floor of your hut," Nickie Sorenson called to her. "We've rolled some big logs around the hut, and they'll stop bullets." He added hastily, "I'm not trying to scare you. These are Tom's orders."

"Thank you," Nelia said. "I don't suppose you would tell me what this means?"

"Not without Tom saying to. I'm sorry."

Nelia put a hand on his pleadingly. "It means more to me than just curiosity," she said earnestly.

Nickie Sorenson went through a struggle with himself; then he snorted, "I know it does, and there's no reason why you shouldn't know. The thing isn't a secret any more, because we've been found."

"What do you mean—who found you?"

"Name of the man who hired you to take those aerial photographs of this jungle was Bottorff? That right?"

"Yes, Albert Bottorff. A big blond man with a beard, who is head of the Magellan and Amazon Petroleum Corporation, of Maracaibo."

Sorenson laughed grimly. "I doubt if Bottorff told you the Magellan and Amazon isn't a South American outfit at all. It's European. It's owned in central Europe, lock, stock and barrel. And I don't need to tell you what that means, with this war over there. It means they're losing everything to the Americans, and fighting like hell to keep it." Sorenson suddenly waved an arm to indicate all the jungle around them. "Did you know the Magellan and Amazon concern had a concession on all this territory? And that they won't develop it, and also won't turn it over to somebody who will, although they've legally broken their drilling time provisions. And that Tom Sail can get the concession if he wants it?"

"No," Nelia said. "I didn't know any of that."

"What we've been doing is running geology on the concession to see if we want it," Nickie Sorenson explained grimly. "No sense of our taking it unless there are good oil formations. Bottorff is naturally trying to stop us."

"Then Fierst—the cross-eyed man was sent by Bottorff to stop Tom?"

Nickie Sorenson looked at her levelly.

"Yes. You were, too," he said.

"I was?" Nelia felt blank.

"Bottorff hired you to take aerial photographs in hopes the pictures would show the location of Tom's camp. We knew that. And we've understood that you didn't know it."

Nelia stared at him, troubled. "Nickie, is that—is this what stands between Tom and myself?"

"No," Nickie Sorenson said promptly. "It isn't."

"Then—"

"I'm not going to tell you that. It is Tom's business. It's something that happened to him, and telling you wouldn't straighten it out."

He walked away then, and there was nothing for Nelia to do but go to her hut. She spent a night that was full of tension, not sleeping at all.

A PLANE LANDED almost as soon as there was light for the pilot to see the small clearing. It was a high-wing cabin job. Nelia, who knew planes, eyed it dubiously. It was so small.

All eight of them loaded aboard. Nelia knew instantly that the plane would not quite take off with that many. And the pilot found it out, too, after he had made a short jolting run. He cut the motor, locked the wheel brakes; the ship skidded to a stop dangerously close to the wall of jungle.

"We'll have to make two trips," said Tom Sail. "If I got out, could you make it?"

"I think so," the pilot muttered.

"Then try it," Tom Sail said quietly. Then a strange expression came to his face. "Wait. Hold the ship a minute." He walked to his thatched *anthitl.*

It seemed a long time that Nelia waited in the plane. Then Tom Sail came back and handed Sorenson a small envelope.

She felt herself trembling when Tom Sail said goodbye, but he spoke none of what she could see in his eyes. He just said, "Goodbye."

The plane left the ground and leaned over and climbed, and the round thatched *anthitls* of the camp grew smaller and quickly became lost in the haze. The jungle was a lush green fur, hiding all that was in it. Nelia sat and choked the arms of the seat with her fingers.

Nickie Sorenson's shout across the aisle startled her. "Here. Tom wanted me to give you this. He didn't say when." He put an envelope into her hands.

She tore across the folded paper in getting it out of the envelope. The paper was a little grimy. Also there was a check, signed with his name, made out to her, the amount blank. She had to hold the two parts together while she read.

Dear Nelia:

There is a good chance that I may not see you again. I have told Nickie Sorenson to see that you get first class passage on the first liner going north. I want you to fill out the enclosed check for the amount your plane cost. I did not know what it cost, but I think I have enough money in the bank.

You see, I shot down your plane. You didn't know that, did you? The leak in your gasoline tank was made by a bullet I fired. It does no good now to say that I did not know it was a woman in the plane, but thought it was someone Bottorff had hired, someone like Fierst. I didn't know until I got back to camp and heard the news broadcasts on the radio. Then we went back to hunt you, Nickie Sorenson and I.

I might have killed you. I have suffered the tortures of a thousand damned whenever I thought of it, which was each minute. Being all ripped up inside, I hardly knew what to think or do.

I love you. I caused you all that suffering and horror in the jungle, so I know you will hate me. All I can say is that the prospect of remaining here is almost pleasant, because I doubt if I care very much about living without you.

Good luck.

Tom Sail.

Nelia clutched at Nickie Sorenson's arm and he winced. "Nickie, why did he write me this?"

"Probably because he figured he wouldn't be alive," said Nickie grimly.

Nelia's eyes widened. "What do you mean?"

"Fierst's men were around the camp. Tom had a man trail them, remember? They were there all last night. They were afraid to attack, because we were too many for them. But now there's just Tom Sail and two others left in camp. And Tom is the man who has been offered the concession. They get him, and they're safe."

Nelia leaped up. Sorenson stopped her. "What are you thinking of doing?"

"I'm going back."

Sorenson blanched. "You insane woman!" he shouted. "You can't!"

THE CLEARING WHICH held the six round thatched *anthitls* of the camp was very still and empty in the brazen sunlight. Nelia sloped the plane down fast, then ruddered from side to side—fishtailing, they called it—to kill speed. The ship bumped the ground, and was chased by a cloud of dust.

He hadn't known how much she loved him—she loved him so much, she thought exultantly, that nothing could stand between them. But because she saw no one about the camp, she could hardly breathe. The plane came to a stop.

"Tom," she cried wildly, and sprang out of the plane. "Oh, Tom, where are you?"

Fierst stepped out of a hut, and the sight of him froze her.

But then Tom Sail stepped out, too. He walked with Fierst toward her, the two men striding through the morning sunlight with no visible restraint between them.

Tom Sail seemed hardly able to restrain his delight at seeing Nelia. "Things didn't turn out as bad as they looked," he told her. "We've become friends."

"That's hardly enough explanation," said the cross-eyed hardwood Fierst amiably. "The fact is, I hope I'm a man of courage myself, and I admire it in others. After Tom Sail upset our applecart yesterday, as neat as you please, I got to thinking. I got to thinking that courage like that deserved a lot. So I decided the hell with this job I'm trying to do. The hell with a fat rabbit from Europe named Bottorff. We Americans, North and South, should get together." Fierst added in a voice that was slyly amused, "I wasn't sure we could lick him, anyway."

"Then, Tom, you're safe?" Nelia breathed.

"He's safe, and falling into good hands, I believe." Fierst was looking at her, and at him, with a South American gentleman's intense pleasure at discovering a romance. "Well, well, myself and my men had better be getting along."

WHEN all the others had retired discreetly, and they stood

beside the plane, Tom Sail spoke: "Nelia, why did you come back?"

"Because I love you."

"But there is something you don't know. I handed Nickie Sorenson a letter—" He was speaking with great strain, and he bogged down.

"He gave me the letter, Tom. And I read it."

"Then you—" A joy leaped into his voice, such a joy that had not been there at any time since she had known him. "Then you still love me—you do. Oh, Nelia, my darling." Suddenly his lips were pressing hers.

"Besides," Nelia said, "this will teach you to always tell me the whole truth and nothing but the truth. I think it's been excellent training for you as a husband."

Two Kukulcans

WHEN SEAWORTHY SMITH first saw Sidonie Hall, he did something without thinking. He ran his fingers through his hair. Later, after certain events, he could think back and discern a reason, a mighty logical reason, for that absent gesture. He must have, that once, been given sufficient clairvoyant powers to tell in advance that Sidonie Hall was going to get in his hair. She and her Kukulcans.

Seaworthy Smith had been enjoying the isolation which his atrocious pipe had secured on the yacht club balcony. He was also worrying, not very feverishly, but none the less worrying. The thing bothering him was the very fact that he was having a moderately good time there by himself. The human is a social animal, Seaworthy had hitherto believed, and he wondered what could be wrong. In '31 he had been a budding advertising man in New York. That the depression had nipped his bud was beside the point. He had acquired *Sot*, the little double-ended cutter, and in the ensuing three years had managed to shove into quite a few of the world's out of the way places, alone. Alone! Hell, that was it! He was turning into an old man of the sea.

"Hafta do somethin''bout this," Seaworthy grumbled and added as punctuation a hiccough.

The hiccough was the key that unlocked the door of enlightenment. Seaworthy Smith had a slight edge on, for he had just been initiated into a quaint Cuban custom that went something like this: A waiter shoved a glass of champagne into your hand, and you stood up and drank it while everybody sang the local version of, "He's a Jolly Good Fellow." You drank it without coming up for air. Then you had the privilege of naming the next victim, and you also named the size of the glass. That last was the catch. Whoever had named Seaworthy Smith had selected a glass that could not have held much less than half a keg. While it had been excellent champagne, Seaworthy was on the balcony because he thought it might be a good idea. Incidentally, the fact he saw Sidonie Hall was no indication the champagne had sharpened his vision. Sidonie Hall was easy to see anywhere.

They must have seen each other at about the same time, although this completely missed Seaworthy Smith at the moment. Had Sidonie Hall been an actress, she no doubt would have starred, for she showed by no sign that Seaworthy Smith was her goal, and that she had found her goal. She separated from her party and vanished shortly in that realm where dissocialization from some half of those present was simply effected by the legend, *Señoritas*. Perhaps the isolation percentage exceeded half, men being in marked majority at this particular stage of the Havana festivities, the trophy presentation and dance marking the end of the annual St. Petersburg-Havana yacht race. Seaworthy Smith had sailed *Sot* single-handed in the race, and had just escaped securing a firm hold on last place.

What Seaworthy Smith did not know was that Sidonie Hall had gone to a telephone, and that she was saying things which would have made him, figuratively, batten down all hatches and rig a storm trys'l.

Having called her party, Sidonie Hall asked, "Leon?" Apparently it was Leon, for she announced, "He's here."

"Bueno!" enthused a basso the receiver reproduced rather well. "Great! Very excellent!"

Sidonie Hall smiled brightly at the telephone, and declared, "He looks as if he would be hard to kill."

"He would be," agreed the basso. "Very hard. I tried it, once."

"That's the kind of a collaborator we *may* need," Sidonie Hall leaned confidingly close to the transmitter's black gullet. "I called to tell you he's here, and you can stop looking for him. This Seaworthy Smith looks like just what we ordered. Now I'm going in and work on him. What's his vulnerable point, Leon?"

"He hasn't any," Leon said positively.

"He has," corrected Sidonie Hall. "They all have. I'll find it. I'll use technique on him, Leon. You savvy technique?"

"Sure. Technique. Oil of the old banana. Same thing. *Mucho bueno!*"

"I hope so," murmured Sidonie Hall. "I think I'll mention lightly, very lightly, the point about all three of us standing a chance of getting shot."

"Mention it heavily," suggested Leon. "He would like that."

"Thanks."

SEAWORTHY SMITH SAW Sidonie Hall next with the Skipper of the *Sikes*, which vessel was the Coast Guard cutter that had mothered the race fleet to Havana. The Skipper must have escaped the local custom of champagne, since he was sober. Sidonie Hall had him in tow, and had him primed— Seaworthy put on his best wooden face when he realized this— to introduce her. Sidonie Hall had a bright metallic evening bag clamped under her left elbow and a full glass in each hand.

The Skipper proved that he had the form for making introductions down pat, then went away.

Sidonie Hall favored Seaworthy with a smile that was nothing if not radiant. "Do you always live in a desert?" she asked, and extended one of her drinks.

Seaworthy was high enough to take the glass, and sober enough to try not to notice the disturbing shape of her as seen against the light from the banquet room. As an aid to not noticing, he struggled mentally and managed to start thinking of a blow which *Sot* had hit off Navidad Banks on the way from Gibraltar, when there had been a crimson sunset so breath-taking as to make him, at the time, wonder distractedly if all Domdaniel really might be coming with the west wind that was so strong it sucked the air out of his lungs. It dawned on him that it was her hair, the brass of it in the light, that was making him think of that sky off Navidad.

He managed to murmur, "Spinnaker weather," with fair success, and put his upper lip into what was in the glass. A daiquiri.

Sidonie Hall waved generally and declared, "Everyone here is boaty. You own *Sot*, don't you?"

Seaworthy nodded carefully, it having come to him that this might be a good time to be stingy with words.

"*Sot* is the cutter which came in seventh, isn't she?" Sidonie Hall asked.

"A double-ender. Twenty-eight feet. Marconi rigged." Seaworthy said this much carefully.

"Only twenty-eight feet," Sidonie Hall murmured, as if she did not consider this a respectable length for a life-boat.

"*Sot* has been across and back three times," Seaworthy

declared with a bit of indignation, being moved to uphold the worth of his vessel as any true sailor would.

"*Sot* must have something," said Sidonie Hall.

Praise his boat and you usually warm a sailor's heart, but this time something went wrong. Probably the blame rested with the champagne. Seaworthy concluded her tone hinted that he did not have much, if any, of the quality usually designated as "something." He began to feel more indignant.

Sidonie Hall now demonstrated that she had done research on the subject of Seaworthy Smith.

"You wrote a book," she said. "It was about wind ships, and women. You laid into the women, what I mean." Little mirth noises escaped her. "I haven't laughed so since the Titanic sank."

Seaworthy's indignation attained proportions. Being filled with the independence which had come of three years of Utopian seafaring, he decided to put her in her place.

He muttered, "Pardon me. I think *Sot* may be dragging her hook," and started off.

He had to stop because she got his arm, and he felt just dizzy enough to suspect that, if she yanked, he would upset.

"Something on your mind?" he asked, trying to make it a growl.

"You bet there is." She motioned with her drink. "I like to scheme in the dark."

He accompanied her—she virtually led him—to the gloomy end of the veranda where, with their presence, they dislodged a pair of neckers.

"You are entered in the race back to Key West?" she asked in a manner which indicated she had looked at the entry list and knew he was not.

"No," Seaworthy said, and fished for his pipe. "Figured on going native for a while."

He managed to get tobacco and fire in his pipe, then hid his face with smoke. The tobacco unfailingly made those who borrowed any of it dizzy, the weed being in the nature of a dire trick which a certain Irish peat bog played on the tobacco plant. Seaworthy Smith had stuffed *Sot's* spinnaker bag with it after the crossing of last winter, the time when they had said nothing the size of *Sot* would make it, and when the spinnaker had iced up and gone in a norther, making the bag available.

Inside the club, they were still singing their local version of, "He's a Jolly Good Fellow." The words of group singing are always hard to understand, and this was no exception, because it was in Spanish. Out here on the balcony, it sounded like:

Oon-cha-la-la! Oon-cha-la-la!

The same thing over and over again.

Seaworthy managed to warm up his indignation again.

"You got something on your mind?" he demanded. "Or have you?"

A click sounded from where the girl's hands probably were, and paper rustled. Brilliance then came out of the glass eye of a small flashlight which had been in her handbag. Seaworthy Smith neglected to look at the article on which she played the light, being intrigued by interesting possibilities that might account for the presence of a little fat revolver which he could see in her bag. The newspaper clipping she wanted him to read had been handled.

EXPLORERS RETURN

Paul Anston Hall, archaeologist of note, and his daughter, Sidonie, were among the passengers on the S.S. *Fruitland*, which docked in Havana today. Hall had to be moved from the S.S. *Fruitland* on a stretcher, a victim, his daughter explained, of a tropical fever contracted in Nicaragua.

Hall and his daughter were returning from an expedition in search of Mayan relics. They were forced to abandon the project because of Hall's illness.

Seaworthy Smith was just far enough from being his usual self to smell a mouse.

"How come that's in English?" he demanded accusingly. "They speak Spanish here."

"Havana has an English newspaper," Sidonie Hall snapped.

"Oh," Seaworthy said, feeling he had pulled a dumb one.

More calmly, Sidonie Hall said, "The tropical fever the clipping mentions my father as having came out a rifle. The bullet had been put to soak in pickled fer-de-lance heads."

"You must make nice friends," Seaworthy grunted. He then burned the end of a finger trying to sink the fire in the bowl of his pipe.

Sidonie Hall put clipping and flashlight with the revolver, closed the bag. "It was a mess. We tried to keep it quiet. We had natives working, of course. But Dad sent them hunting while we dug the things out, cleaned them off, made sure what they were, and packed them. But the men must have watched, and one deserted. That was on the trek to the coast. Probably he got word to Coliaz. In fact, we are sure of it now. Leon said he was sure, too. We had almost reached the coast when Coliaz and some of his men jumped us."

Seaworthy Smith jerked his pipe out of his teeth, having suddenly discovered his potent tobacco did not seem to mix with champagne in quantities.

"Coliaz was killed," Sidonie Hall went on. "Our men, of course, fled. We expected that. Except Leon. He stuck. We ran, too, and did some shooting. Dad was hit, but we did not learn until later about the bullet being pickled. Dad was weak. I was not much better. Leon had our packs. We lost Leon. Finally, we reached a port and got aboard the *Fruitland*."

Seaworthy Smith snorted. "And none of this got out because Nicaragua has nice hot jails with bugs, I suppose."

"You're swacked," gritted Sidonie Hall.

"Who? Me?"

Sidonie Hall became dictatorial. She poked Seaworthy's chest with a finger.

"I'm going to bring Leon to talk to you," she declared, "when you sober up."

Seaworthy Smith now became speechless. One of the numerous reasons why he had bought *Sot* and gone to sea was the boss of the advertising agency, who had a habit of poking people in the chest and telling them what he was going to do. Seaworthy had never choked a woman, but he was contemplating it when Sidonie Hall whirled and tapped her heels away.

HAVANA WAS EXPERIENCING one of Cuba's periodic descents of martial law. The curfew was half past one in the morning, after which hour anyone found on the streets could be assured of spending the rest of the night in jail. The champagne had made Seaworthy Smith cautious, so at promptly one o'clock, he stood on the dock, frowning at a red-headed young woman and saying, "You, again!"

"Sobered up?" Sidonie Hall demanded.

"One generally sobers down," Seaworthy informed her.

Sidonie Hall waved attention to the answer to a female's prayer who stood at her elbow.

"This is Leon," she announced.

Seaworthy Smith looked at Leon. Seaworthy then swallowed twice with difficulty, after which he put on his wooden face.

Leon was husky and brown and nice enough to contemplate. He had pale patches in front of his ears, as if he had recently dispensed with sideburns. His English was good, his politeness great.

"I am delighted to meet you," Leon said, not looking at all delighted.

"Hmmm," said Seaworthy Smith, eyeing Leon intently.

"Let's go aboard and talk," Sidonie Hall suggested.

Knocking around outlandish ports is an instructive course in caution. The proper thing now was to say No. Firmly. No. *No!*

"Yes," said Seaworthy Smith, proving possibly no lesson is ever thoroughly learned.

Sot's dinghy was a pet idea of Seaworthy's. The dink was designed to fit over the skylight when at sea, and it gave the cabin both protection and darkness. The dink was ridiculously small, and when they had safely gained *Sot's* deck, it was with an air of having accomplished something. Seaworthy unlocked the cabin hatch, swung down, popped a match on a thumbnail and applied it to the kerosene lamp which hung in gimbals. The one berth was full of sails so they distributed themselves on two sacks of coconuts and an unopened can of copper bottom-paint.

"Do you remember what was in the clipping and what I told you?" asked Sidonie Hall.

Seaworthy Smith frowned down at Sidonie Hall's ankle, which was a nice ankle.

"Is there a second installment to the thriller?" he growled.

Leon took up the conversation and murmured, "It is no thriller. Not now. But it had its moments. I had to hide those packs from Coliaz's men. They were too heavy to carry. I buried the packs. I did not mark the place, but I could find it again."

Seaworthy turned down the lamp, which had a habit of burning too high soon after being lighted.

Leon continued, "I came to Havana and managed to find Miss Hall."

Sidonie Hall said, "If we can get back to the Nicaraguan coast, Leon could dig up the packs. It will not be dangerous unless Coliaz's friends catch us."

"Who was Coliaz?" Seaworthy asked.

"The Liberator," Leon exhibited his white teeth grimly. "The Nicaraguan woods are full of Liberators. Coliaz was a bandit, a bad *hombre*."

Sidonie Hall furthered enlightenment by adding, "Coliaz left friends with political pull. The revenge brand of political publicity goes over with the natives. It is not popular for Americans to shoot a local hero, even in defense of their lives and property."

Seaworthy Smith listened to the harbor waves hitting *Sot's* hull, with sounds somewhat like eggs being dropped.

Sidonie Hall looked over as much of *Sot's* interior as she could see from where she sat on the coconut bag. "This boat looks awfully small."

"She's sound!" Seaworthy grunted.

"She looks terribly uncomfortable," Sidonie Hall declared. Seaworthy put out his jaw and growled, "*Sot* passed a trans-Atlantic liner hove-to in a blow off Montauk."

Leon was beginning to look pleased. He had nodded vehement agreement both times Sidonie Hall had slammed *Sot*.

"These are facts which I pointed out to Miss Hall previously," Leon declared. "*Sot* is hardly fit for our purpose. We should have a larger, faster, and more comfortable boat."

"With a boat like that, you'd be sure to get caught," Seaworthy told them knowingly. "What you want is a little hooker, a yacht, which Coliaz's friends will not suspect. That's what you've got to have. That's what I've got here."

Sidonie Hall sighed resignedly, "How much?"

Seaworthy looked into Sidonie Hall's very blue eyes, which she promptly began using for a bargain argument. He had, however, already made up his mind.

"Nothing," he said.

Sidonie Hall looked stunned. "What?"

"Not a cent," said Seaworthy. "I'll take you for nothing."

Leon jumped up and yelled, "There's something funny about this!"

"You should know," Seaworthy told him.

Leon sat down again, looking very much like a midwesterner eating his first snails.

Sidonie Hall seized Seaworthy's hand and pumped it violently. "We can shove off as soon as we take aboard stores in the morning."

The ship's clock on the bulkhead clanged its bell three times. Sidonie Hall looked at the clock and hastily rescued her hand.

"It's half past one!" she shrieked.

"I know," Seaworthy agreed.

"But the curfew!"

"You can stay aboard," Seaworthy dismissed that problem.

"There's only one berth."

Seaworthy Smith began gathering up blankets and cushions, announcing, "Leon and I can sleep in the cockpit, can't we, Leon?"

Leon nodded, looking as if he were in the latter stages of being devoured by some inner monster of gloom.

They spread the cushions and blankets on the seats at either side of the cockpit where they could sleep, providing they did not mind their feet entangling the steering wheel spokes. Leon was settled by the time Seaworthy made his own pallet and closed the cabin hatch. Seaworthy then went over and leaned close to Leon.

"What's the gag?" Seaworthy whispered.

Leon lay still for a moment, then breathed, "A strange thing is Fate. Two years ago, was it not?"

"Three," corrected Seaworthy. "What became of your brother?"

Leon hesitated. "He is still in Spain."

Seaworthy leered in the darkness and demanded, "In jail?"

Leon must have swallowed with difficulty, because he made a clucking noise. "Oh, no. He is—in business."

"Hmmm."

Leon murmured apologetically, "It is not pleasant to be without money in Spain. A foreigner, an American, with his pockets lined from the Monte Carlo tables. My brother and I were young and reckless. It was a bad combination."

Seaworthy blew hot breath in Leon's face. "You and that brother got the tar whaled out of you trying to rook me. After that there was some talk about the next time we met."

"That is all in the past," Leon muttered.

"Yeah?" Seaworthy sighed. "I just wondered."

Leon whispered, "Why did you agree to take us for nothing?"

Seaworthy considered that at some length.

"I like to fuss with that gal," he said finally.

Leon was silent. Seaworthy waited for some moments for him to speak. Then he leaned down.

"You watch your step, pal!" Seaworthy advised.

Leon maintained his silence.

Sidonie Hall surprised Seaworthy by failing to bring aboard the two or three suitcases and the hatbox with which the gentler sex usually start a small boat cruise. She had one canvas duffle bag.

IN THE CARIBBEAN the next evening, the sun left them with a swell and little wind. *Sot* began the acrobatics of which a twenty-eight footer is capable. Sails slatted; the traveler made noise. At two bells, it was dark.

Seaworthy let the wheel spin by itself, and was below half an hour, during most of which time the alcohol stove made its usual hissing. He came on deck with corned beef in which he had fried onions and potatoes.

Leon got one whiff of the concoction, promptly lay down on the deck runway, and his torso heaved.

"You have a swell sense of humor," Sidonie Hall informed Seaworthy. "You knew what would get him down."

Seaworthy searched his mind for a suitable remark, found it barren, went below and emptied sardines out of a paper bag.

He presented the bag to Leon with the suggestion: "Breathe in it for a while. Puts carbon dioxide in you or something."

Leon breathed industriously into the bag, then let it fall overboard and float away, after which he did not again have mal de mer. Whether this was due to the remedy or not was open to argument.

"How'll we divide the watches?" Sidonie Hall wanted to know.

"I'll take it all night," Seaworthy declared. "I'm used to single-handing."

Leon slept on deck. Seaworthy turned the wheel over to Sidonie Hall at dawn, and she was teaching Leon to steer a compass course when he went below to turn in. She had sailed before, he could tell. He lay and listened to her voice until he discovered what he was doing, then peered cautiously through the hatch and made sure they could not see below. He now searched Leon's bag, being careful to notice how things came out. A big single-action revolver with a pearl grip and a box of cartridges, partially empty, proved to be his objective. He slept little that morning, for it was a tedious job twisting the lead out of the cartridges so as to leave the soft metal unmarked. Even though he padded the pliers, he ruined two of the cartridges, but these might not be missed since the box was not full, anyway.

The repacking of Leon's bag he did painstakingly, putting each article back as he had found it.

THE MAINS'L SLAMMING over in a jibe aroused him in the afternoon, and he bounded on deck before coming fully awake, so it was just as well that he had turned in with clothes on.

"You gotta be careful about that!" he yelled.

The tropical sun had made Sidonie Hall red. She had been eating graham crackers and the heat had baked the brown paste which these had left on her lips. Also, she was now wearing Seaworthy's best slacks. Seaworthy glared when he discovered she had snipped several inches off each leg.

"I was steering when the sail changed sides," Leon said, looking somewhat flustered. "I had no idea it would go over so violently."

"Be careful next time," Seaworthy growled, feeling thwarted.

"I will," Leon promised.

Seaworthy frowned as he took the reading of the patent log, which he had streamed the night before. He went below to make figures on the margin of Navy Hydrographic chart 1290. His dot of position was not far off the course from Havana to the spot on the Nicaraguan coast where Leon had stated the packs were buried.

IT BLEW AROUND midnight. Sidonie Hall came up, unsummoned, to take the wheel while Seaworthy tied in a reef. She was, he had to admit, good. She luffed up enough to give slack for tying the reef points, but not so much that the boat lost steerage way.

Leon also came up, but did not stir from the cockpit. He looked worried throughout. Seaworthy took the wheel, studied Leon for some time, then deliberately mishandled the boat so that she took a wave over the bow.

Leon cried out, grabbed the cockpit rail. Seaworthy began to wear a satisfied look, as if he had just settled something in his own mind.

"You better go below and get in oilskins," he bellowed at Leon.

Leon dived below with the wind worrying his dark hair.

"You've sailed before," Seaworthy yelled in Sidonie Hall's ear.

Her laugh sounded as if she were enjoying herself. "Dad and I once took a forty-five foot schooner to the Galapagos to look at some stone statues."

Seaworthy started to speak, but the wind filled his mouth and made him cough.

"Haven't you any bump of curiosity?" Sidonie Hall shrieked at him unexpectedly.

"You mean about the packs?" he shouted back. "It's a secret, isn't it?"

"There are two Kukulcans in the packs," she screamed. "Images. They weigh probably seventy-five pounds apiece. The workmanship is fascinating."

"Gold?"

"Simon pure."

Seaworthy opened his mouth, but the wind got in again.

Leon came on deck. He had secured himself a life preserver.

"I wonder what good you think that would do?" Seaworthy growled, but Leon did not hear because of the wind.

It was calm again in an hour.

Sidonie Hall cooked breakfast and burned Seaworthy's eggs, but had amazingly good luck with those for Leon and herself. From a log reading and a frowning inspection of the compass, Seaworthy made more figures on the chart edge.

"Don't you know celestial navigation?" Sidonie Hall demanded.

"Yes," Seaworthy growled. "Do you?"

"Saint Hilaire and I are old pals," she said calmly.

Seaworthy hoped he did not look startled. Lying in his berth, he rubbed his jaw thoughtfully and not because he needed a shave. The chronometer was in gimbals at the head of the berth, where it could not be seen from the cockpit. He spent an hour making figures on a piece of paper, after which he carefully changed the time of the chronometer.

SIDONIE HALL USED Seaworthy's sextant to take latitude and longitude shots the next day, and he saw but pretended to sleep. When she had figured her results, he let her see that he was awake.

"We've got it right on the nose," she announced.

Seaworthy went to sleep wearing a smile of peace, but he secretly changed the chronometer again the following morning, after more figuring. After resetting the chronometer, he lay for a time and listened to Sidonie Hall and Leon in the cockpit discussing Coliaz.

Deceased Coliaz, it seemed, had made a specialty of foreigners, from the States preferably, which might explain his popularity among the natives.

Further sailing did not improve fellowship aboard. Leon became morose, and did as little work as he could. Sidonie Hall, on the contrary, showed entirely too much life. Once, she almost caught Seaworthy fiddling with the chronometer.

THEY SIGHTED LAND at night, and Seaworthy took *Sot* in fairly close to let go the heavy anchor on the fly so that it would bite in. Leon helped get the dink off the skylight. Seaworthy produced a shovel from the lazaret under the cockpit, explaining, "Use it to dig clams sometimes."

Leon entered the cabin, then came out stuffing his six-shooter in his pants' waistband. He was more surly than usual. He focused Seaworthy's binoculars on the shore for some time. "It is hard to tell," he complained. "From here the shore looks different."

"I got a shot at Sirius half an hour ago and plotted a Sumner line," Seaworthy assured him, "We're not over a mile from where I wanted to be."

There was a subdued enthusiasm in everyone's manner as Seaworthy sculled them in. But this was dampened somewhat when the lively dink inadvertently swamped in the surf. They hauled the small, water-filled boat up on the beach sand, the water not having been much more than knee-deep when they swamped.

It was hard work tilting the dink to empty it of water, and suddenly Leon ceased helping and jumped to one side.

Sidonie Hall gasped audibly. She became rigid. The moon-light was sufficient to show that she had made fists of her hands.

Seaworthy let the dink drop back and growled, "I had a hunch this was coming."

"Coliaz was my brother!" Leon shouted, then promptly screamed again, *"Coliaz was my brother!"*

"You haven't got the nerve, Leon," Seaworthy said. "You figured if you got us to Nicaragua, you could escape after you avenged your honor, or whatever you call it. Only it won't work. This isn't Nicaragua."

"What?" Leon squalled.

"This is Yucatan!" Seaworthy snapped.

Leon began shaking. He used both hands to hold his gun.

Waves lunged at the beach, fell into suds and noise, then the water ran back in a thin sheet dotted with foam flecks. The sand almost got dry after the water left and before it came again. Footprints and other marks which they had made dragging the dink had lost character and were joining the limbo of things which have been and are no more, and to which, somehow, it was not cheering to give thought.

Leon gritted, "The girl has been taking our position!"

"I changed the chronometer every day," Seaworthy explained. "That threw her calculations off."

"I have friends in Yucatan," Leon snarled.

"Was afraid of that," Seaworthy sighed. "So I also took the powder out of your cartridges."

During the pause that ensued, the waves came several times.

"I am going to pull the trigger!" Leon said, a pronounced hoarseness in his voice.

Seaworthy growled, "Go ahead. Then I'm going to do some pulling myself."

Seaworthy wheeled slowly and started forward. Queerly enough, he found time to be surprised at how much he had to force himself.

Leon emitted something choking and inarticulate. Then he threw his gun in the sand and ran away. He went fast, making those rather confounding sounds of a grown man who is crying.

Seaworthy Smith stopped, wheeled and looked at Sidonie Hall in the moonlight. Sidonie Hall was not nearly as grateful as he not unreasonably expected.

Sidonie Hall gasped, "The Kukulcans!"

"Gone." Seaworthy made a gesture of throwing something away. "Leon undoubtedly got rid of them right away."

If Sidonie Hall was expected to show grief, she did not run to form. She shook her fist at Seaworthy Smith and shrieked, "You—you barnacle! You never made the slightest effort to find out about my Kukulcans. You didn't care about them."

"Nope," Seaworthy admitted cheerfully.

Impulse got the better of her, and she took a swing at him. The dictates of self defense demanded that Seaworthy trap her with both arms, after which the unexpected happened, as it sometimes does. In discussing it later, they never did quite figure out the exact psychological cycle which occurred. Anyway, Seaworthy abruptly decided she was not the headstrong baggage which he had been trying all along to tell himself she was. She was, in fact, darn sweet.

After a while, Seaworthy, for no good reason that he could later discern, felt the urge to pick up Leon's revolver and demonstrate that it was indeed quite empty. He pointed it casually and purely by chance at the dink and pulled the trigger.

There was an explosion that both deafened and startled him, not to mention what it did to his dignity. A bullet hole came into the bottom of the dink.

"I remember now," Seaworthy gulped eventually. "I forgot the shells in the gun."

Luck

THE FISH TREMBLED its tail as the knife cut off its head, then red ran out of it and made a mess on the planks and spread enough to cover the wet red marks where two human hands had tried to hold to the dock edge.

Sail put the palm of his own hand in the mess.

The small policeman came from shore. He had shoved through the small green gate with the discreet sign, *Private Yachts—No Admittance*, at the shore end of the swanky pier, and was under the neat green canopy, tramping in the rear edge of the glare from his flashlight. His leather and brass glistened in the light. He was cautious enough to walk in the middle of the narrow long pier, but did enough stamping with his feet to show he was the law.

When he reached Sail, he stopped. His cap had a cock. His lower lip was loose on the left side, as if depressed by a pipe stem that wasn't there. He was young, bony and brown.

He asked, "That you give that yell?"

Sail picked up the hook and wet line. He held the hook close to his left palm. He grimaced at the small oozing rip in the brown callus of the palm. It was about the kind of a hole the fishhook would have made.

"Yeah?" the cop said vaguely. "You snagged the hand on a hook, eh? Made you yell?" The policeman toed the fish head's open mouthful of snake-fang teeth.

"Barracuda," he said, but not as if that was on his mind.

Red drops came out of the ripped palm, fattened on the lower edge, came loose and fell on the dock. Sail picked the fish up with his other hand. When he stood his straightest, he was still shorter than the small cocky policeman.

The officer splashed light on Sail. He saw the round jolly brown features of a thirtyish man who probably liked his food, who would put weight on until he was forty, and spend the rest of his life secretly trying to take it off. Sail's hair might have been unraveled rope, and looked as if it had been finger-combed. Some of the black had been scrubbed out of his black polo shirt. Washings had bleached his black dungarees; they fitted his small hips tightly and stopped halfway below the knees. Bare feet had squarish toes. Weather had gotten to all of the man a lot.

The officer hocked to clear his throat. "They don't eat barracuda in Miami. Not when you catch the damn things in the harbor, anyhow."

He didn't sound as if that was the thing bothering him, either.

Sail asked, "You the health department?"

The little policeman filled Sail's eyes with light. He said, "If that was a crack—" and changed to, "Was it you yelled?"

"Any law against a yell when you get a hook in your hand?"

The policeman popped his light into Sail's face again. Derision was around Sail's blue eyes and in the warp of his lips.

Loud music was coming from the moonlight excursion boat at the south end of the City Yacht Basin, but a barker spoiled the effect of the music, if any. Two slot machines alongside the lunch stand at Pier Six ate sailor nickels and chugged away.

A hundred million dollars' worth of yachts within a half-mile radius, the Miami publicity bureau said. Little Egyptian-silk-sail racing cutters that had cost a thousand a foot. A big three-hundred-foot Britisher, owned by Lady Something-or-other who only had officers with beards. And in-between sizes. Teak, mahogany, chromium, brass. Efficiency. Jap stewards as quiet as spooks. Blond Swede sailors. Skippers with leather faces, big hands and great calm.

The policeman pointed his flashlight beam at the boat tied to the end of the dock. The light showed the sloping masts, the black canvas covers over the sails, the black, neat, new-looking hull. Life preservers tied to the mainstays had *Sail* on them in gold leaf.

"What you call that kind of a boat?" the cop asked.

"Chesapeake five-log bugeye," Sail said. "Her bottom is made out of five logs drifted together with Swedish iron rods. The masts on bugeyes always rake back like that. She's thirty-four feet long in the water. You'll have trouble beating a bugeye for knocking around shallow water, and they're pretty fair sea—"

"Could it cross the ocean?"

"She has."

"Yeah? My old man's got the crazy idea he wants to go to the South Seas. He's nuts about boats."

"It gets you."

"This one yours?"

"Yes," Sail said.

"How old is it?"

"Sixty-eight years old."

"T'hell it is! That's older'n my old man. I don't think he'd want it."

"She'll take you anywhere," Sail defended.

"What's she worth?"

"Seventy-five thousand dollars," Sail said.

The policeman whistled. Then he laughed. He did not say anything.

Sail said, "There are some panels in the cabin, genuine hand carvings by Samuel McIntire of Salem. Probably they were once on a clipper ship. That's what makes her price stiff."

The cop did not answer. He switched off his light.

"All I can say is you let out a hell of a funny yell when you catch a fish," he said.

He took pains to stamp his feet while he walked away. By the time Sail got the effects of the flashlight out of his eyes, the officer was out of sight.

SAIL HELD HIS hands close to his chest, fingers spread, palms in. There was barely enough breeze to make coolness against one side of his face. The music on the moonlit sailboat stopped. The barker was silent. Over in the Bayfront Park outdoor auditorium a political speaker was viewing something with alarm. After he had felt his hands tremble for a while, Sail went to his boat.

The boat, *Sail*, rode springlines at the dock end. She had a thirty-four-foot waterline. Twelve-foot beam, two-foot draft with centerboard up, seven with it down. She was rigged to be sailed by one man, all lines coming aft.

The interior was teak, with inset panels of red sanders, fustic and green ebony, all hand-carved by a man who had died in 1811. How Samuel McIntire panels came to be in the bugeye, Sail did not know, but he had been offered a thousand dollars for each year of age for the boat and was hungry broke when he turned it down. It was not a money matter. Some men love dogs.

Sail slapped the fish into a kettle in the galley and, hurrying, put most of his right arm through a porthole, grasped a line, took half hitches off a cleat, and let the line go. The line snaked quietly down into the water, following a sinking live-box and its contents of live fish and crawfish.

Sail looked out of the hatch.

The young policeman had come quietly back to where the fish had bled and was using his flashlight. He squatted. After a while, he approached the dock end, moseying. Too carefully. When his flashlight brightened the bugeye's black masts and black sail covers, Sail was in the galley, making enough noise cutting up the fish to let the cop know where he was and what he was doing.

Sail waited four or five minutes before putting his head out of the hatch. The cop had gone somewhere silently.

Sail was still looking and listening for the policeman when he heard the man's curse and the woman's cry, short, sharp. The man's curse was something of a bray of surprise. The sounds came out of Bayfront Park, between the waterfront yacht basin and Biscayne Boulevard. Sail, not stirring, but watching the park, saw a man running among the palms. Then the young policeman and his flashlight were also moving among the palms.

During the next five minutes, the policeman and his flash were not still long enough for him to have found anything.

Sail stripped naked, working fast once more. His body was rounding, the hair on it golden and long, but not thick. He looked at his belly as if he didn't like it, slapped it and sucked it in. The act was more a habit than a thought. He put on black jersey swim trunks.

Standing in the companion looking around, Sail scratched his chest and tugged the hair on it. His fingers twisted a little rattail of the chest hair. No one was in sight. He got over the side without being too conspicuous about it.

The water had odor and the usual things floated in it. He swam under the dock, searching. The tide was high slack, almost, but still coming in just a little, so things in the water were not moving away.

The pier had been built stout because of the hurricanes. There was a net of cross timbers underneath, and anything falling off the south side of the dock would drift against them. Sail found what he was seeking on the third dive.

He kept in the dark places as he swam away with it.

THE LITTLE ISLAND—ARTIFICIAL, put there when they dredged the harbor—was darkly silent when Sail swam laboriously toward it. Pine trees on the island had been bent by the hurricanes, and some torn up. The weeds did not seem to have been affected.

Sail tried not to splash as he shoved through the shallows to the sand beach. He towed the Greek underwater. Half a dozen crabs and some seaweed clung to the Greek when Sail carried him into the pines and weeds. The knife sticking in the Greek, and what it had done, did not help. The pines scratched and the weeds crunched under the Greek when Sail laid him down. It was very dark.

Pulpy skins in a billfold were probably greenbacks, and stiffer, smaller rectangles, business cards. Silver coins, a pocket knife, two clips for an automatic. The automatic holster empty under the Greek's left armpit. From inside the Greek's coat lining, another rectangle, four inches wide, five times as long, a quarter of an inch thick. It felt like hardwood. The Greek's wristwatch still ticked.

Sail put the business cards and the object from the coat lining inside his swim trunks, and was down on his knees cleaning his hands in the sand when the situation got the best of him. By the time he finished being sick, he had sweated profusely.

The water felt cold as he swam back the way he had come— under the docks and close to the seawall—with the Greek.

Sail clung to *Sail's* chain bobstay until all the water had run off him that wanted to run off, then swung aboard and moved along the deck, keeping below the wharf level, and dropped down the hatch. He started to take the bathing suit off, and the girl said, "Puh-lease."

She swung her legs off the forward bunk. Light from the kerosene gimbal lamp did not reach all of her. The feet were small in dark blue sandals which showed red-enameled toenails. Her legs had not been shaved recently, but were nice.

Pink starting on Sail's chest and spreading made his tan look dark and uncomfortable, and he chewed an imaginary something between his large white front teeth as he squinted at the girl. He seemed about to say something two or three different times, but didn't, and went into the stateroom and got out of the swim trunks. The shadow-wrapped rest of her did not look bad as he passed. He tied a fish sinker to the trunks and dropped them through a porthole into the bay, which was dredged three fathoms deep here. He put on his scrubbed black clothes.

The girl had moved into the light. The rest of her was interesting.

"You probably think I'm a tart," she said. "I'm not, and I wish you'd let me stay here awhile longer. I have a good reason."

Sail scratched behind his right ear, raised and lowered his eyebrows at her, stalked self-consciously into the galley, pumped freshwater in a glass and threw it on the galley floor, then stepped in it. His feet now left wet tracks such as they had made when he came aboard. He seemed acutely conscious that his efforts to make this seem a perfectly sensible procedure were exaggerated. His hands upset a round bottle, but he caught it. He set it down, picked it up again, asked:

"Drink?"

She had crossed her legs. Her skirt was split. "That would be nice," she said.

Sail, his back to her, made more noise than necessary in rattling bottles and glasses and pinking an opener into a can of condensed milk. He mixed two parts of gin, one of crème de cacao, one of condensed milk. He put four drops from a small green bottle in one drink and gave that one to the girl, holding it out a full arm length, as if he didn't feel well acquainted enough to get closer, or didn't want to frighten her away.

They sipped.

She said, "It's not bad without ice, really."

"I did have an electric ice box," he told her, as if excusing the lack of ice. "But it and this salt air didn't mix so well."

Her skirt matched her blue sandals, and her yellow jersey was a contrast. Her long hair was mahogany, and done in a bun over each ear, so that her long oval face had a pure, sweet look. She drank again. Her blue leather handbag started to slip out of the hollow of her crossed legs and she caught it quickly.

Sail put his glass down and went around straightening things which really didn't need it. He picked up the *News* off the engine box. It was in two parts. He handed one part to the girl. That seemed to press the button. She threw the paper down and grabbed her blue purse with both hands.

"You don't need to be so goddamn smart about it!" she said through her teeth.

She started to get up, but her knee joints did not have strength, and she slid off the bench and sat hard on the black battleship linoleum. Sail moved fast and got his plump hands on the blue purse as she clawed it open. A small bright revolver fell out of the purse as they had a tug-of-war over it.

"Blick!" the girl squealed.

BLICK AND A revolver came out of the oilskin locker. The gun was a small bright twin to the girl's. Blick's Panama fell off slick mahogany hair, and disarranged oilskins fell down in the locker behind him. Blick had his lips rolled in until he seemed to have no lips. He looked about old enough to have fought in the last war.

"Want it shot off?" he gritted.

Sail jerked his hand away from the girl's purse as if a bullet was already headed for it. He put his hands up as high as the cabin carlins and ceiling would allow. His mouth and eyes were round and uneasy, and the upper part of his stomach jumped a little with each beat of his heart, moving the polo shirt fabric.

Blick gave Sail a quick search. He was rough. His lips were still rolled in, and a sleeve was still jammed up on one arm, above a drop of blood that was not yet dry.

The girl started to get up, couldn't. She said, "Blick!" weakly.

Blick, watching Sail, threw at her, "You hadda be a sucker and drink with him!"

The girl's lips worked over some words before sounds started coming. "... was ... I ... know he ... it doped?"

Blick gritted at Sail, "Bud, she's my sis, and if she don't come out of that, I wouldn't wanta be you. Help me get her goin'!"

Blick dropped his sister's purse and gun in his coat pocket, got his Panama, then took the girl's right arm, letting Sail look into the little gun's muzzle all the while. "Help me, bud!"

Sail took his hands down. Sweat wetness was coming through his washed black polo shirt. He watched Blick's eyes and face instead of watching the gun. They walked the girl up the companion and onto the dock. Blick put his hand and small revolver into a trouser pocket.

"We're tight. Stagger!"

They staggered.

The orchestra on the moonlit excursion boat was still trying to entice customers for the moonlight sail. Yacht sailors, some of them with a load, stood in a knot at the end of the lunch stand, and out of the knot came the chug of the slot machines. Blick was tall enough to glare over his sister's head at Sail. His glare was not bright.

"What'd you give her?"

Sail wet his lips. The sweat had come out on his forehead enough to start running.

"Truth serum."

"You louse!"

Two sailors, one without his shirt, went past, headed for the slot machines.

Blick said, "Bud, I think I got you figured. You're a guy Andopolis rung in. He'd still try to get a boat and another guy."

Sail squinted out of one eye. Perspiration was stinging the other.

"Andopolis was the one who didn't digest the knife?"

"You ain't that dumb!"

"Was he?"

"You know that was Abel!"

Sail said, "Believe it or not, I'm guessing right across the board. Abel was to do the dirty work while you and the girl hung around on shore. Abel tried to take something from Andopolis on the dock. Abel had something that had something to do with whatever he wanted. He tapped it inside his coat as he talked. Abel got knifed, let out a bellow, and went off the dock into the drink. Andopolis ran after he knifed Abel. You headed him off in the park. He got away and ran some more. You did a sneak to my hooker while the cop looked around."

"Did you guess all that?" Blick sneered.

They were nearing Biscayne Boulevard and traffic. On the *News* building tower, the neon sign alternately spelled *WIOD* and *NEWS*. Sail took a deep breath and tried to watch Blick's face.

"I'd like to know what Abel wanted."

Blick said nothing. They scuffed over the sidewalk, and Blick, walking as if he did not feel as if he weighed much, seemed to think to a conclusion which pleased him.

"Hell, Nola. Maybe Andopolis didn't spill to our bud, here."

Nola did not answer. She seemed about asleep. Blick pinched her, slapped her, and that awakened her somewhat.

A police radio car was parked at the corner of Biscayne and

Blick did not see it in time. He said, as if he didn't give a damn, "Stagger, bud! This should be good."

Sail shoved a little to steer the girl to the side of the walk farthest from the prowl car. Blick shoved back to straighten them up. The result was that they passed close enough to the police machine to reach it with one good jump. Sail shoved Blick and Nola as hard as he could, using the force of the shove to propel himself toward the car. He grabbed the spare tire at the back and used it to help himself around the machine to shelter.

Blick's revolver went off three times about as rapidly as a revolver could fire. Both cops in the car brayed, and fell out of the car onto Sail.

Blick carried Nola to a taxicab forty feet down the street, and dumped her in. He stood beside the hack, aimed, and air began leaving the left front tire of the police car. The cops started shooting in a rattled way. Blick leaped into the taxi. An instant later, the hack driver fell out of his own machine, holding his head. The taxi took off. The two cops sprang up, and piled into their machine, one yelling:

"What about this one in the street?"

"Hell, he's dead."

The cops drove after the taxi, one shooting, his partner having trouble steering with the flat tire.

Sail, for a fat man, ran away from there very fast.

SAIL PLANTED HIS heaving chest against the lunch stand counter, held on to the edge with both hands, and stood there awhile, twice looking down at his knees and moving them experimentally, as if suspecting something was wrong with them. The young man, who looked as youths in lunch stands somehow always manage to look, came over and swiped the counter with his towel.

"What've you got in cans?" Sail asked him, then stopped the answering recital on the third name. Beer suds overflowed the can before it hit the counter. Sail drank the first can and most of the next in big gulps, but slowed down on the third and seemed tied up in thought. He scraped at the tartar on a tooth with a fingernail, then started chewing the nail and got it down to the quick, then looked at it as if surprised. He absently put three dimes on the counter.

"Forty-five," the youth corrected.

Sail added a half dollar and said, "Some nickels out of that."

He carried the nickels over to the mob around the slot machines. He stood around with his hands in his pockets. He tried whistling, and on the second attempt got a good result, after which he looked more satisfied with himself. His mouth warped wryly as he watched the play at the two machines. He took his nickels out, looked at them, firmly put them back, but took them out a bit later. When there was a lull, he shoved up to the slot machines.

The one-armed bandit gave him a lemon and two bars, with another bar just showing.

"You almost made it," someone said. "A little more and you'd have made the jackpot."

"Brother," Sail said, "you must be a mind reader."

He backed up, waited, still giving some attention to his private thoughts, until he got a chance at the other machine. It showed a bar, a lemon, a bar. Sail rubbed his forearms, looked thoughtful and walked off.

A telephone booth was housed at the end of Pier Four. Sail, when a nickel got a dial tone, dialed the 0, said, "Operator, I believe in giving all telephone operators possible employment, so I never dial a number. Give me police headquarters, please." He waited for a while after the operator laughed, said, "I want to report an attempted robbery," then told someone else, "This is Captain Sail of the yacht *Sail*. A few minutes ago, a man and a woman boarded my boat and marched me away at the point of a gun. I do not know why, except that the man was a drug user. I feel he intended to kill me. There was a police car parked at the corner of Biscayne, and when I broke away and got behind it, the man tried to shoot me, then drove off with the woman in a taxi, and two officers chased them. I want to know what to do now."

"It would help if you described the pair."

The man and woman Sail described would hardly be recognized as Blick and Nola.

"Could you come up to headquarters and look over our gallery?" asked the voice.

"Where is it?"

"Turn left off Flagler just as you reach the railroad."

When Sail left the telephone booth, the youth with the hot-dog-stand look was jerking the handle of one slot machine, then the other, and swearing.

"Funny both damn things blew up!" he complained.

Sail walked off wearing a small secret grin.

TWO HOURS LATER, Sail pushed back a stack of gallery photographs in police headquarters and said in a tired, wondering voice, "There sure seem to be a lot of crooks in this world. But I don't see my two."

The captain at his elbow said heartily, "You don't, eh? That's tough. One of the boys in the radio car got it in the leg. We found the taxi. And we'll find them two. You can bet on that." He was a big brown captain with the kind of jaw and eyes that went with his job. He had said his name was Rader.

Sail rode back to the City Yacht Basin in a taxi, and looked around before he got out. He walked to *Sail*. While adjusting a springline, he saw a head shape through the skylight. By craning, he saw the head shape was finished out by a police cap. Sail walked back and forth, changing the springlines, which did not need changing, and otherwise putting off what might come. Finally, he pulled down his coat sleeves, put on an innocent look and went down.

One policeman waiting in the cabin was using his tongue to lather a new cigar with saliva. The tongue was coated. He was shaking, not very much, but shaking. His face had some loose red skin on it, and his neck was wattled.

The second policeman was the young bony cop with the warp in the end of his mouth. He still had his flashlight.

The third man was putting bottles and test tubes in a scuffed brown leather bag which held more of the same stuff and a microscope off which some of the enamel was worn. He wore a fuzzy gray flannel suit, had rimless, hookless glasses pinched tight on his nose, and had chewed up about half of the cigar in his mouth without lighting it. The cigar was the same kind the other policeman was licking.

Sail said, "I just talked to Captain Rader."

The warp got deeper in the end of the young cop's mouth. He switched his flashlight on and off in Sail's eyes, then hung it from the hook on his belt.

"What about?"

Sail told them what he had talked to Captain Rader about—the kidnapping, which he said he could not understand. In describing Nola and Blick, whom he did not name—he made no mention of having heard their names—he repeated the words he had used over the telephone.

When it was over, the young cop stepped forward, jaw first.

"All right, by God! *Now you can tell us the truth!*"

The shaking policeman got up slowly, holding his shiny damp cigar and looking miserable. "Now, Joey, that way won't do it."

Joey grabbed Sail's right wrist and squeezed it. "The hell it won't! Lewis says there was human blood on the dock along with the fish blood!"

The shaking policeman said, "Now, Joey."

Joey shouted, "A lot of people heard somebody let out a yip. Even over in the park where I was doing the vice squad's work, I heard it."

Sail held out his left hand to show the tear in the brown callus of the palm.

"A fishhook made that," he said. "You saw it bleed. There's your human blood on the dock."

Joey yelled, "Mister sailor, we've been checking on you by radio. You cleared from Bimini, the customs tells us. We radioed Bimini. You know what? You were asked to get out of Bimini. A gambling joint went broke in Bimini because one of their wheels had been wired and a lot of lads in the know made a cleaning. It ended up in a brawl and the gambling joint owner went to the hospital."

Joey shook his finger at Sail's throat. "The British police asked around and it began to look as if you had tipped the winners how to play. The joint owner claimed he didn't know his wheel was wired. It ended up with you being asked to clear out. The only reason you're not in the Bimini jug is because they couldn't figure any motive. You didn't get a cut. You hadn't lost any jack on the wheel. You didn't have a grudge against the owner. It was a screwy business, the British said, from beginning to end. But that's what they think. I think different. You know what I think?"

"I doubt if it would be interesting," Sail said dryly.

"I think you outfoxed 'em. You're a smooth article. That's what you think. But you can't pull this stuff here."

The shaking policeman said, "You haven't got a leg, Joey," between teeth clicks.

"I'll sweat the so-and-so until I got a thousand legs!"

The freezing policeman groaned, "You should have your behind kicked, Joey."

Joey released Sail's right wrist to frown at the other officer. "Listen, Mister Homicide—"

The shaking policeman got between Joey and Sail and stood there, saying nothing. Joey frowned at him, then sucked at his lower lip, pulling it out of shape.

"Hell, if you gotta run this, run it!" he said.

He turned and stamped up the companion, across the deck and, judging from the sounds, had some kind of an accident and nearly fell overboard getting from the boat to the dock, but finally made it safely.

The other policeman, grinning without much meaning in it, extended a hand which, when Sail took it, was hot and unnatural. After he held the hand a moment, Sail could feel it trembling.

"I'm Captain Chris of homicide," the officer said. "I want to thank you for reporting your trouble to Captain Rader, and I want to congratulate you on your narrow escape from those two. But next time, don't take such chances. Never fool with hop and guns. We'll let you know as soon as we hear anything of your attacker and his girl friend or sister, whichever she was. I hope you have a good time in Miami in the meantime. We have a wonderful city. Florida has a wonderful climate." He shook with his chill.

The rabbity man, Lewis, who had not said anything, finished putting things in his bag, picked up a camera with a photoflash attachment which had been unnoticed on a bunk, and went up the companion, stepping carefully, as one who was not used to boats. He got onto the dock carefully with bag and camera. Captain Chris followed.

Sail said, "Quinine and whiskey is supposed to be good for malaria. But only certain quinines."

"Thanks," said Captain Chris. "But I think whiskey gave it to me."

They walked away, and young Joey was the only one who looked back.

The tide stood at flood slack, the water still, so that things did not float away. Something bright was bobbing on the water, and Sail got a light. He found five of the bright things when he hunted. Used photographic flashlight bulbs, with brass bases not corroded enough by the salt water for them to have been in long. Sail went below and looked around. Enough things were out of place to show the hooker had been searched. Fingerprint powder had not been wiped off quite well enough.

SAIL CATNAPPED ALL night, sleeping no more than a half hour soundly at any one time. He spent long periods with a mirror which he rigged to look out of the companion without showing himself.

On a big Matthews cruiser tied across the slip, somebody was ostensibly standing anchor watch. Boats lying at a slip do not usually stand on anchor. The watcher did not smoke and did not otherwise allow any light to get to his features. It was dark enough that he might have been tall or short, wide or narrow. The small things he did were what any man would do during a long, tiresome job, with one exception.

He frequently put a finger deep in his mouth and felt around.

Party fish boats making noise on their way out of Pier Five furnished Sail with an excuse to go on deck at about six bells. He stood there yawning, rubbing his head with his palms and making faces. He rubbed a finger across his chest and rolled up little twists and balls of dirt or old skin, after which he took a shower with the dock hose.

The watcher was not around the Matthews in the morning sun. Sail went below to don a pair of black shorts which washing had faded.

Sail's dinghy rode in stern davits, bugeye fashion, at enough of a tilt not to hold seas or spray, and Sail lowered it. He got a brush and the dock hose and washed down the topsides, taking off dried salt that seawater had deposited on the hull. He dropped his brush in the water three different times; it sank, and he had to reach under for it.

The third time he reached under for the brush, he retrieved the stuff which the Greek's clothing had yielded the night before. The articles had not worked out of the nook between the dock cross braces underwater where Sail had jammed them after swimming back from the island where he had taken the dead Greek.

Sail finished washing down, hauled the dink up on the davits, and during the business of coiling the dock hose around the faucet in the middle of the dock, he worked his eyes. Any one of a dozen staring persons within view might have been the watcher from the Matthews. The other eleven would be tourists down for a gawk at the yachts.

Sail took the Greek's stuff out of the dink when he got the scrub brush. He went below. Picking the business cards apart was a job because they were soaked to pulp. He examined both sides of each card as he got it separated. One card said Captain Santorin Gura Andopolis of the yacht *Athens Girl* chartered for Gulf Stream fishing and that nobody caught more fish. The address was Pier Five. *I live aboard*, was written in pencil on the back.

The other twenty-six cards said the Lignum Vitae Towing Company had a president named Captain Abel Dokomos. The address was on the Miami River, and there was a telephone number for after six.

The piece of board was four by twenty by a quarter inches, mahogany, with screw holes in the four corners. Most of the varnish was gone, peeled rather than worn off, and so was some of the gold leaf. There were a letter and four figures in gold leaf:

K 9420

Sail burned all of the stuff in the galley Shipmate.

A man was taking two slot machines away from the lunch

stand as Sail passed on his way uptown. Later, he passed four places which had slot machines, and there was a play around all of them. Sail loafed around each crowd, but not as if he wanted to. He walked off from one crowd, then came back. In all, he managed to play three machines. The third paid four nickels and he played two back without getting anything. The slot in a dial telephone got one of the surviving nickels.

He told the operator he didn't dial as a matter of principle and asked for Pier Five, and when he got Pier Five, asked for Captain Santorin Gura Andopolis of the *Athens Girl*. It took them five minutes to decide they couldn't find Captain Andopolis.

After the telephone clanked its metal throat around the fourth nickel, Sail repeated the refusal to dial and asked for the number of Captain Abel Dokomos' Lignum Vitae Towing Company.

When he heard the answer, he made his voice as different as he could. "Cap'n Abel handy?"

"He hasn't come down this morning. Anything we can do?"

"Call later," Sail said.

The woman on the other end of the wire had been Blick's sister Nola, visitor aboard *Sail* the night before.

SAIL SELECTED A cafeteria which was a little overdone in chromium. The darkie who carried his tray got a dime. There was a small dab of oatmeal on the first chair Sail started to sit on. He broke his egg yolks and watched them run with an intent air. The fifth lump made his coffee cup overflow. He put almost a whole egg down with the first gulp from the force of habit of a man who eats his own cooking and eats it in solitude.

A boy wandered among the tables, selling newspapers and racing tip sheets. He carried and sold more tip sheets than newspapers. Sail took the coffee slowly with the spoon, getting a little undissolved sugar out of the bottom of the cup with each spoonful, seeming to enjoy it. The sugar lumps were wrapped in paper carrying the cafeteria's advertisement, and he unwrapped one and ate it after he finished everything before him. He put the papers in the coffee cup.

The man in a stiff straw hat eating near the door did not put syrup or anything sweet on his pancakes or in his coffee. And when he finished eating, he poked the back of his cheek absently with a finger, then put the finger in the back of his mouth to feel.

Sail got up and took a slow walk until he came to a U-Drive-It. There was a slot machine in the U-Drive-It. He tried it, and it paid off only in noise. He made a deposit and got a light six-cylinder sedan. For three blocks, he drove slowly, looking out and appraising buildings for height. He picked one much taller than the others and parked in front of it. After starting into the building, he came back to look over an upright dingus, one of a row of the things along the curb. Small print said motorists could park there half an hour if they put a nickel in the dingus and turned the handle.

"The whole town's got it," he complained, and shook the device to see if it would start working without a nickel. It wouldn't and he put one in.

He said loudly, just before entering one of the tall building elevators, "Five!"

The fifth-floor corridor was not much different from other office building corridors. There were three real estate and one law office and some more.

The man who had felt his bad tooth in the cafeteria came sneaking up the stairs from the fourth floor and put his head around the corner. Sail was set. The man's straw hat sounded surprisingly like glass when it collapsed, and the man got down on all fours to mew in pain. Sail hit again, then unwrapped his belt from his fist. He blew on the fist, working the fingers.

"I've got to rush my friend to a place for treatment," he told the operator when the elevator cage came.

He thanked the operator and half a dozen other volunteer assistants while he started the rented car. He drove past the U-Drive-It. The proprietor was fussing with his machine.

Sail drove five or six miles by guess before he found a lonesome spot and got out. He hauled the man out. Sail's breathing was regular and deeper than usual; his eyes were wide with excitement, and he perspired. He wiped his palms on his clerical black shorts and bent over his victim.

The man with the bad tooth began big at the top and tapered. His small hands were callused, dirt was ground into the calluses, and the nails were broken. He had dark hair and a dark face, but got lighter as he went down, finishing off with feet in a pair of white shoes. He smelled a little as men smell who live on small boats with no baths.

His pockets held three hundred in nothing smaller than tens, all new bills, in a plain envelope. There was a dollar sixty-one in silver mixed up with the cashier's slip for his cafeteria breakfast. In ten or so minutes, he was scowling at Sail.

He said something in Greek. It sounded like his personal opinion of Sail or the situation.

Sail said, "Andopolis?"

"You know my name, so whatcha askin' for?" the man growled without much accent.

"You're here because I been getting too much attention," Sail said. "That oughta be clear, hadn't it?"

Andopolis felt his head, that part of his cheek over his bad tooth, then got to his feet. Sail took his belt out of his pocket and started threading it through the loops. Andopolis clutched his head, groaned, started to sit down, but jumped at Sail instead. Sail moved to one side, but not enough, and Andopolis hit his shoulder and the impact turned him around and around. Andopolis hit him somewhere else, and the whole front of his body went numb and something against his back was the ground.

"I'll stomp ya!" Andopolis yelled.

He jumped on Sail with both feet, and Sail was still numb enough to feel only the dull shock. His rounded body rolled under the impact, and Andopolis waved his arms to keep erect. Sail had his belt unthreaded. He laid it like a whip across Andopolis' face. Andopolis grabbed his face, and was wide open when he sat down heavily beside Sail.

WHEN ANDOPOLIS CAME to, his wrists were fastened with the belt. Sail had his shirt unbuttoned and was examining the damage the other's feet had done. There was one purple print of the entire bottom of Andopolis' right foot, and a skinned patch where the other had slid off, with loosened skin tangled in the long golden hairs, but not much blood. He put back his head and shoulders and started to take a full breath, but broke it off in coughing. He sat down coughing, holding his chest, and sweated.

"Yah!" Andopolis gloated. "I stomp your guts good if you don't lay off me! What you been follerin' me for?"

Sail looked up sickly. "Followin' you?"

"Yah."

Sail, still sitting, said, "My Christian friend, you stood anchor watch on me last night. You haunted me this morning. But still I was following you, was I?"

"Before that, I'm talk about," Andopolis growled. "You follow me to Bimini in that black bugeye. I make the run from Bimini here yesterday. You make it too. What kinda blind fool you take me for? You followin' me, and don't you think I don't know him."

"It must have been coincidence."

"Don't feed me, mister."

"It just might be that nobody will have to feed you for long."

"Whatcha mean?"

"You were walking down the dock toward my boat last night when Abel jumped you. You sort of ruined Abel, and I covered up for you, but that's not the point. The point is, why were you coming to see me?"

"Aw, hell, I was gonna tell you about followin' me."

Sail coughed some, deep and low, trying to keep it from moving his ribs, then got up on his feet carefully.

"All right, now we're being honest with each other, and I'll tell you a true story about a yacht named *Lady Luck*."

Andopolis crowded his lips into a bunch and pushed the bunch out as far as he could, but didn't say anything.

Sail said, "The *Lady Luck,* Department of Commerce registration number K 9420. She belonged to Bill Lord of Tulsa. Oil. Out in Tulsa, they call Bill the Osage Magician on account of what he's got that it seems to take to find oil. Missus Bill likes jewelry, and Bill likes her, so he buys her plenty. Because Missus Bill really likes her rocks, she carries them around with her. You following me?"

Andopolis was. He still had his lips pooched.

"Bill Lord had his *Lady Luck* anchored off the vet camp on Lower Matecumbe last November," Sail continued. "Bill and the missus were ashore, looking over the camp. Bill was in the trenches himself, and is some kind of a shot with the American Legion and the Democrats, so he was interested. The missus left her pretties on the yacht. Remember that. Everybody has read about the hurricane that hit that afternoon, and maybe some noticed that Bill and his missus were among those who hung on behind that tank car. But the *Lady Luck* wasn't so lucky, and she dragged her pick off somewhere and sank. For a while, nobody knew where."

Sail stopped to cough. He had to lie down on his back before he could stop, and he was very careful getting erect. Perspiration had most of him wet.

"A couple of weeks ago, a guy asked the Department of Commerce lads to check and give him the name of the boat, and the owner, that carried number K 9420," Sail said, keeping his voice down now. "The word got to me. Never mind how. And it was easy to find you had had a fishing party down around the Matecumbes and Long Key a few days before you got curious about K 9420. It was a little harder to locate your party. Two guys. They said you anchored off Lower Matecumbe to bottom-fish, and your anchor fouled something, and you had a time, and finally, when you got the anchor up, you brought aboard some bow planking off a sunken boat. From the strain, it was pretty evident the anchor had pulled this planking off the rest of the boat, which was still down there. You checked up as a matter of course to learn what boat you had found."

Andopolis looked as if more than his tooth hurt him.

Sail kept his voice even lower to keep his ribs from moving.

"Tough you didn't get in touch with the insurance people instead of contacting Captain Abel Dokomos, a countryman who had a towing and salvage outfit and no rep to speak of. You needed help to get the *Lady Luck*. Cap Abel tried to make you cough up the exact location. You got scared and lit out for Bimini. You discovered I was following you, and that scared you back to Miami. You wanted a showdown, and when Cap Abel collared you on the dock as you were coming to see me, you took care of that part of your troubles with a knife. But that left Abel's lady friend, or whatever she is, and her brother, Blick. They were in the know, too. They tried to grab you last night in the park after you fixed Abel up, and you outran them. Now, that's a very complete story, or do you think?"

Andopolis was a man who did his thinking with the help of his face, and there was more disgust than anything else on his features.

"YOU TRYIN' TO cut in?" he snarled.

"Not trying."

"Then what—"

"Have."

The sun was comfortable, but mosquitoes were coming out of the swamp around the road to investigate.

"Yeah," Andopolis said. "I guess you have, maybe."

Sail put his shirt on, favoring his chest. "We've got to watch the insurance outfit. They paid off on Missus Bill's stuff. Over a hundred thousand. They'll have wires out."

Andopolis got up and held out his hands for the belt to be taken off, and Sail took it off. Andopolis said, "I thought of the insurance when I got Cap Abel. We used to run rum. The Macedonian tramp!"

"There's shoal-water diving stuff aboard my bugeye," Sail said.

"You don't get me in no water! Shark, barracuda, moray, sting rays. Hell of a place. If I hadn't been afraid, I'd have done the diving myself. I thought of that, believe me."

"That's my worry. It's not too bad, once you get a system." Sail felt his chest. "I guess maybe these ribs will knit in a while."

Andopolis looked much better, almost as if he had forgotten his tooth. "It's your neck. O.K. if you say so."

"Then let's get going."

Andopolis was feeling his tooth when he got into the car. Sail had driven no more than half a mile when both front tires let go their air. The car was in the canal beside the road before anything could be done about it.

THE CAR BROKE its windows going down the canal bank. The canal must have been six feet deep, and its tea-colored water filled the machine at once. Sail had both arms over his middle where the steering wheel had hit. So much air had been knocked out of him, and his middle hurt so, that he had to take something into his lungs, and there was only water. He began to drown.

The water seemed to be rushing around inside the car,

although there was room for no more to come in. Sail couldn't find the door handles. The broken windows he did find were too small to crawl out of, but after exploring three, he got desperate and tried a small one. There was not enough hole. He pushed and worked around with the jagged glass, his head out of the car, the rest of him inside, until strange feelings of something running out of his neck made him know he was cutting his throat.

He pulled his head in, and pummeled the car roof with blows that did not have strength enough to knock him away from what he was hitting. It came to his mind to try the jagged glass again as being better than drowning, but he couldn't find it, and clawed and felt with growing madness until he began to get fistfuls of air. He sank twice before he clutched a weed on shore, after which the spasms he was having kept him at first from hearing the shots.

Yells were mixed in with the shot sounds. Andopolis was on the canal bank, running madly. Blick and his sister were on the same bank, running after Andopolis, shooting at him, and having, for such short range, bad luck. They were shooting at Andopolis' legs. All three ran out of sight. Sound alone told Sail when they winged Andopolis and grabbed him.

Sail had some of the water out of his lungs. He swam to a clump of brush which hung down into the water, got under it, and managed to get his coughing stopped by the time Blick and Nola came up hauling Andopolis. Andopolis sobbed at the top of his voice.

"Shoot his other leg off if he acts up, Nola," Blick yelled. "I'll get our little fat bud."

Sail wanted to cough until it was almost worth getting shot

just to do so. Red from his neck was spreading through the water under the brush.

"He must be a submarine," Blick said. He got a stick and poked around. "Hell, Nola, this water is eight feet deep anyhow."

Andopolis babbled something in Greek.

Blick screamed, "Shut up, or we'll put bullets into you like we put 'em into your car tires!"

Andopolis went on babbling.

"His leg is pretty bad, Blick," Nola said.

"Hell, let 'im bleed."

Air kept coming up from the submerged car. Sail tried to keep his mind off wanting to cough. It seemed that Blick was going to stand for hours on the bank with his bright little pistol.

"He musta drowned," Blick said. "Get that other leg to workin', Andopolis. You didn't know we been on your trail all night and all mornin', did ya? We didn't lose it when this Sail got you, either."

Andopolis whimpered as they hazed him away. Car sound departed.

CAPTAIN CHRIS, WIDE-EYED and hearty and with no sign of a chill, exclaimed, "Well, well, we began to think something had happened to you."

Sail looked at him with eyes that appeared drained, then stumbled the other two steps down the companion into the main cabin of *Sail* and let himself down on the starboard seat. Pads of cotton under gauze made Sail's neck and wrists three times normal thickness. Tape stuck to his face in four places, and iodine had run out from under one of the pieces and dried.

Young bony Joey looked Sail over and his big grin took the warp out of the corner of his mouth.

"Tsk, tsk," he said cheerfully. "Somebody beat me to it."

Sail gave them a look of bile. "This is a private boat, in case you forgot."

"He's mussed up and now he's tough!" Joey said. "Swell!"

"Now, now, let's keep things on an amiable footing," Captain Chris murmured.

Sail said, "Drag it!"

Joey popped his palms together, aimed a finger at Sail. "You got told about Lewis finding human blood in that fish mess on the dock last night. But try to alibi the rest. There was wet tracks in this boat. That was all right, maybe, only some of the tracks were salt water and the water spilled on the galley floor was fresh. We got the harbor squad diver down this morning. He found a box on the bottom below this boat with live fish in it. He found a bathing suit with a sinker tied to it. And this morning, a yachtsman beached his dink on the little island by Pier One and found a dead Greek. We sat down with all that and done our arithmetic, and here we are."

Sail's face began changing from red and tan to cream and tan, although the bandages took away some of the effect.

Captain Chris said, "Joey, you'd make a lousy gambler, on account of you show your cards."

Sail said in a low voice, "You're gonna get your snouts busted if you keep this up!"

Captain Chris looked unconvincingly injured. "I didn't think we'd have any trouble with you, Mister Sail. I hoped we wouldn't. You acted like a gentleman last night."

Sail had been seated. He got up, bending over first to get the center of gravity right. He pointed a thumb at the companion. "Don't fall overboard on your way out."

"I bet he thinks we're leaving!" Joey jeered.

A string of red crawled out from under one of the bandages on Sail's neck. His face was more cream than any other color. He reached behind himself into the tackle locker and got a gaff hook, a four-foot haft of varnished oak with a bright tempered-steel hook with a needle point. He showed Joey the hook and his front teeth.

He said violently, "I've got a six-aspirin headache and things to go with it! I feel too lousy to shy at cops. You two public servants get the hell out before I go fishing for kidneys."

Joey yelled happily, "Damn me, he's resisting arrest and threatening an officer!"

Sail said, "Arrest?"

"I forgot to tell you." Joey grinned. "We're going to—"

Sail asked Captain Chris, "Is this on the level?"

"I regret that it is," Captain Chris said. "After all, evidence is evidence, and while Miami is noted for her hospitality, we do draw lines, and when our visitors go so far as to use knives on—"

"I'm gonna hate to break your heart, you windbag!" Sail said angrily.

He took short steps, and not very fast ones, into the galley, and took the rearmost can of beer out of the icebox. He cut off the top instead of using the patent opener. When the beer had filled the sink with suds, he got a glass tube which had been waxed inside the can. He held out the two sheets of paper which the tube contained.

Joey raked his eyes over the print and penned signatures,

then spelled them out, lips moving.

"This don't make a damn bit of difference!"

Captain Chris complained, "My glasses fell off yesterday during one of them infernal chills. What does it say, Joey?"

"He's a private dick assigned to locate some stuff that sank on a yacht. The insurance people hired him."

CAPTAIN CHRIS BUTTONED his coat, pulled it down over his hips, set his cap by patting the top of it.

"I'm afraid this makes it different, Joey."

Joey snorted. "I say it don't."

Captain Chris walked to the companion. "Beauty before age, Joey."

"Listen, if you think—"

"Out, Joey."

"Mister Homicide, any day—"

"Out!" Captain Chris roared. "You're as big a goddamn fool as your mother."

Joey licked his lips while he kept a malevolent eye on Sail, then took a step forward, but changed his mind and climbed the companion steps. When he was outside, he complained, "Paw, you and your ideas give me an ache."

Captain Chris sighed wearily while he looked at Sail. "He's my son, the spoiled whelp." He hesitated. "You wouldn't want to cooperate?"

"I wouldn't."

"If you get yourself in a sling, it'd be better if you had a reason for refusing to help the police."

Sail said, "All I get out of this is a commission for recovering the stuff. Right now, I need that money like hell."

"You'd still get it if we helped each other."

"Maybe. But I've cooperated before."

Captain Chris shrugged, climbed three of the companion's five steps, and stopped. "This malaria is sure something. I could sing like a lark today, only I keep thinking about the chills due tomorrow. Did you say a special quinine went in that whiskey?"

"Bullards. It's English."

"Thanks." Captain Chris climbed the rest of the way out.

When the two policemen reached the dock, Sail came slowly on deck and handed Captain Chris a bottle. "You can't buy Bullards here."

"Say, I appreciate this!"

"If my day's run of luck keeps on the way it has, you'll probably find your knife man in a canal somewhere," Sail said slowly.

"I'll look," Captain Chris promised.

The two cops went away with Joey kicking his feet down hard on the dock boards.

THERE WAS A rip in the nervous old man's canvas apron, and he mixed his words with waves of a pipe off which most of the stem had been bitten. He waved the pipe and said, "My, mister, you must've had a car accident."

Sail, holding to the counter, said, "What about the charts?"

"Yeah, there's one other place sells the government charts besides us. Hopkins Carter. But if you're going down in the keys, we got everything you need here. If you go on the inside, you'll want thirty-two-sixty and sixty-one. They're the strip charts. But if you take Hawk Channel, you'll need harbor chart five-eighty-three, and charts twelve-forty-nine, fifty and fifty-one. Here, I'll show—"

Sail squinted his eyes, swallowed and said, "I don't want to buy a chart. I want you to slip out and telephone me if either of certain two persons comes in here and asks for chart twelve-fifty, the one which has lower Matecumbe."

"Huh?"

Sail said patiently, "It's simple. You just tell the party you got to get the chart, and go telephone me, then stall around three or four minutes before you deliver the chart, giving me time to get over here and pick up their trail."

The nervous old man put his pipe in his mouth and immediately took it out.

"What kind of shenanigans is this?"

Sail showed him a license to operate in Florida.

"One of them private detectives, huh?" the old man said, impressed.

Sail put a ten-dollar bill on the counter.

"That one's got twins. How about it?"

"Mister, if you'll just describe your parties. That's all!"

Sail made a word picture of Blick and Nola, putting the salient points down on a piece of paper. He added a telephone number.

"The phone's a booth in a cigar store on the corner. I'll be there. How far is this Hopkins Carter?"

"Two blocks."

"I'll probably be there for the next ten minutes."

Sail, walking off, was not as pale as he had been on the boat. He had put on a serge suit more black than blue and a new black polo. When he was standing in front of the elevator, taking a pull at a flat amber bottle which had a crown and a figure 5 on the label, the old man yelled.

"Hey, mister!"

Sail lowered the bottle, started coughing, and called between coughs, "Now"—*cough*—"what?"

"Lemme look at this again and see if you said anything about the way he talked."

Sail moved back to where he could see the old man peering at the paper which held the descriptions. The old man took his pipe out of his teeth.

"Mister, what does that feller talk like?"

"Well, about like the rest of these crackers. No, wait. He'll call you bud two or three times."

The old man pointed his pipe at the floor. "I already sold that man a twelve-fifty. 'Bout half hour ago."

Sail pumped air out of his lungs in a short laugh which had no sound except the sound made by the air passing his teeth and nostrils. He said, "That's swell. They would probably want a late chart for their X-marks-the-spot. And so they've got it, and they're off to the wars, and me, I'm out ten per cent on better than a hundred thousand."

He had taken two slow steps toward the elevator when the old man said, "The chart was delivered."

Sail came around. "Eh?"

"He ordered it over the telephone. We delivered. I got the address somewhere." He thumbed an order book. "*Whileaway.* A houseboat on the river below the Twelfth Street Causeway."

Sail put a ten on the counter. "The brother."

HE WAS A fat man trying to hide a big face behind two hands, a match and a cigar. He said, "Oof!" and his dropping hands dragged cigar ashes down his vest when Sail prodded him in the upper belly with a fingertip.

Sail said, "I just didn't want you to think you were getting away with it."

The fat man turned his cigar down at an injured angle. "With what?"

"Whatever you call what you've been doing."

"There must be some mistake, brother."

"There's been several. It'll be another if you keep on trying to tail me."

"Me, tailing you! Why should I do that?"

"Because you're a cop. You've got it all over you. And probably because Captain Chris ordered me trailed."

The plainclothesman sent his cigar between two pedestrians, across the sidewalk and into the gutter. "Mind telling me what you can do about it?"

Sail had started away. He came back, pounding his heels. "What was that?"

"I've heard all about you, small-fat-and-tough. You're due to learn that with the Miami Police Department, you can't horse—"

Sail put his hand on the fat man's face. The fingers were spread, and against the hand's two longest fingers, the fat man's eyeballs felt wet. Sail shoved out and up a little. The cop did not yell or curse. He swung a vicious uppercut. He kicked with his right foot, then his left. The kicks would have lifted a hound dog over a roof. He held his eyes. The third kick upset a stack of gallon cans of paint.

Sail got out of there. He changed cabs four times as rapidly as one cab could find another.

WHILEAWAY WAS BUILT for rivers, and not very wide rivers. She was a hooker that couldn't take a sea. A houseboat about sixty feet waterline, she had three decks that put her up like a skyscraper. She should never have been built. She was white, or had been.

Scattered onshore near the houseboat was a gravel pile, two trucks with nobody near them, a shed, junk left by the hurricane, a trailer with both tires flat, windows broken, and two rowboats in as bad shape as the trailer. Sail was behind most of them at one time or another on his way to the riverbank. There was a concrete seawall. Between Sail and the houseboat, two gigs, a yawl, a cruiser and another houseboat were tied to dolphins along the concrete river bulkhead. Nobody seemed to be on any of the boats.

Sail wore dark blue silk underwear shorts. He hid everything else under the hurricane junk. The water had a little more smell and floating things than in the harbor. He kept behind the moored boats after he got over the seawall, and let the tide carry him. He was just coming under the *Whileaway* bow when one of the square window ports opened almost overhead.

Sail sank. He thought somebody was going to shoot or use a harpoon.

Something large and heavy fell into the water and sank, colliding with him, pushing him out of the way and going on sinking. He had enough contact with it to tell the first part of it was a navy-type anchor. He swam down after it. The river had two fathoms here, and he found the anchor and what was tied to it. The tide stretched his legs out behind as he clung to what he had found.

Whoever had tied the knots was a sailor, and sailor knots,

while they hold, are made to be easily untied. Sail got them loose.

It would have been better to swim under the houseboat and come up on the other side, away from the port from which the anchor and Nola had been thrown, but Sail didn't feel equal to anything but straight up. His air capacity was low because of his near drowning earlier in the day.

He put his head out of the water with his eyes open and fixed in the direction of the square port. No head was sticking out of the port. No weapon appeared. The tide had taken Sail near the stern of the *Whileaway* and still carried him.

He got Nola's head out. Water leaked from her nose and mouth. Sail got an arm up as high as he could, clutching. He missed the first sagging springline, got the second. The rope with which the anchor had been attached to Nola still clung to her ankles. He tied one of her arms to the springline so that her head was out.

Sail went up the springline with his hands until one foot would reach the window sills. From there to the first deck was simpler.

Nola began to gag and cough. It made a racket.

Sail opened his mouth to yell at her to be quiet. She couldn't hear him yet, or understand. He wheeled and sloped into the houseboat cabin.

The furnishings might have been something once, but that had been fifteen years ago. Varnish everywhere had alligatored.

Sail angled into the galley when he saw it. He came out with a quart brass fire extinguisher which needed polishing, and a rusted ice pick. There had been nothing else in sight.

Nola got enough water out to start screeching.

BEYOND THE GALLEY was a dining room. Sail had half crossed it when Captain Santorin Gura Andopolis came in the opposite door with a rusty butcher knife.

Andopolis was using a chair for a crutch, riding its bottom with the knee of the leg which Blick and Nola had put a bullet through. Around his eyes—on the lids more than elsewhere—were puffy gray blisters about a size which burning cigarettes would make. Three fingernails were off each hand. Red ran from the three mutilated tips on the right hand down over the rusty butcher knife.

Sail had time to throw the fire extinguisher and made use of the time, but the best he did was bounce the extinguisher off the bulkhead behind Andopolis.

Andopolis said thickly, "I feex you up, mine fran!" and deliberately reversed the butcher knife for throwing.

Sail threw his ice pick. It stuck into Andopolis' chest over his heart. It did not go in deep enough to bother Andopolis. He did not even bother to jerk it out.

Sail jumped for the door, wanting to go back the way he had come. His wet feet slipped, let him down flat on his face.

Feet came pounding through the door and went overhead. Sail looked up. The feet belonged to the plainclothes detective who had been in the hardware store which sold marine charts.

Andopolis threw his knife. He was good at it, or lucky. The detective put his hands over his middle and looked foolish. He changed his course and ran to the wall. His last steps were spraddling. He leaned against the bulkhead. His hands did not quite cover the handle of the butcher knife.

Andopolis hobbled to Sail on his chair. He stood on one leg and clubbed the chair. Sail rolled. The chair became two pieces and some splinters on the floor. Sail, still lying on the floor, kicked Andopolis' good leg. Andopolis fell down.

As if that had given him an idea, the detective fell. He kept both hands over the knife handle.

Andopolis used the two largest parts of the chair and flailed at Sail. On all fours, Sail got away. His throat wound was running again. He got up, but there was no weapon except the bent fire extinguisher. He got that. Andopolis hit him with the chair leg and his left side went numb from the belt down. He retreated, as lopsided on his feet as Andopolis, and passed into the main cabin.

Nola was still screaming. A man was swearing at her with young cocky Joey's voice. Men were jumping around on the decks and in the houseboat rooms.

Blick sat on the main cabin floor, getting his head untangled from the remains of a chair. His face was a mess. It was also smeared with blue ink. The ink bottle was upside down under a table on which a new chart was spread open. A common pen lay on the chart.

Andopolis came in following Sail. Andopolis crawled on one knee and two hands.

Blick squawked, "What's Nola yellin' for?"

Andopolis crawled as if he did not see Sail or Blick, had not heard Blick. A tattered divan stood against the starboard bulkhead. Andopolis lay down and put an arm under that. He brought out a little bright pistol, either Blick's or his sister's.

Captain Chris jumped in through the door.

Andopolis' small pistol made the noise of a big one. Blick, sitting on the floor, jumped a foot when there seemed no possible way of his jumping, no muscles to propel him upward. He came down with his head forward between his knees, and remained that way, even after drops began coming out of the center of his forehead.

Captain Chris had trouble with his coattails and his gun. Andopolis' little gun made its noise again. Captain Chris turned around faster than he could have without some help from lead, and ran out, still having trouble with his gun.

Sail worked the handle of the fire extinguisher. The plunger made *ink-sick!* noises going up and down. No tetrachloride came out. There was nothing to show it ever would. Then the first squirt ran out about a foot. The second was longer, and the third wet Andopolis' chest. Sail raised the stream and pumped. He got Andopolis' eyes full and rolled.

Andopolis fired once at where Sail had been. Then he got up on one foot and hopped for the door. His directions were a little confused. He hopped against a bulkhead.

Andopolis went down on the floor and began having a fit. It was a brief fit, ending by Andopolis turning over on his back and relaxing.

The wall had driven the ice pick the rest of the way into his chest.

Outside, Nola still screamed, but now she made words, scatteredly.

"Andopolis ... killing Blick ... tried ... me ... Andopolis ... last night ... Abel ... knife ... we ... him ... tell ... broke loose ... me ... anchor ... Blick ...."

Sail ran to the table. The chart on the table had two ink lines forming a V with arms that ran to landmarks on Lower Matecumbe, and compass bearings were inked beside each arm, with the point where the lines came together ringed.

Sail left with the chart by the door opposite the one which he had come in by, taking the chart. He found a cabin. He tore the V out of the chart, folded it flat and tucked it under his neck bandages, using the stateroom mirror to adjust the bandages to hide the paper. He threw the rest of the chart out of a port on the river side.

CAPTAIN CHRIS WAS standing near dead Andopolis. Torn coat lining was hanging from under the right tail of his coat, but he had his gun in his hand.

"Where'd you go to?" he wanted to know.

"Was I supposed to stick around while you drew that gun?"

"The fireworks over?"

"I hope so."

Captain Chris put his gun in his pants pocket. "You're pinched. Don't say I didn't warn you."

Young Joey came in, not as cocky and not stamping his feet. Two plainclothesmen followed him, then two uniformed officers walking ahead of and behind the old man who sold the charts in the hardware store.

The old man pointed at Sail and said, "He's the one who asked about the feller who ordered the chart. Like I told you, I gave him—"

"Save it." Joey glared at Captain Chris. "We still ain't got nothing on this fat sailor, Paw. The girl says Andopolis is a party fisherman whose anchor pulled up part of a boat."

The girl had told about everything. Joey kept telling the story until he got to, "So Sail yanked the dame out, and now what've we got to hold him on?"

Captain Chris, looking mysterious and satisfied, told Sail,

"Get your clothes on or we'll book you for indecent exposure along with the rest."

"What rest?"

"Get your clothes on."

Sail dressed sitting on the hurricane wreckage, brushed off the bottoms of his feet and put on socks and shoes. He looked up at Captain Chris as he tied the shoestrings.

"Kidding, aren't you?"

"Sure, sure!"

Sail bristled. "You've got to have a charge. Just try running me in on an INV and see what it gets you."

"I've got a charge."

"In a gnat's eye."

Captain Chris said with relish, "You've been playing the slot machines which are so popular in our fair city. You used a slug made of two hollow halves that fit together and hold muriatic or something that eats the works of the machines and puts them on the fritz. We found a box of the slugs on your boat. We have witnesses who saw you play machines before they went bad."

Sail wore a dark look toward the squad car. "This is a piker trick."

Captain Chris tooled the car over a bad street. "You put that gambling joint in Bimini on the bum, too. What's the idea?"

"Nuts."

"Now, don't get that way. I'm jugging you, yes. But it's the principle. It's to show you that it ain't a nice idea to football the cops around. Not in Miami, anyway. You'll get ten days or ten bucks is all. It's the principle. That, and a bet I made with Joey that if he'd let me handle this and keep his mouth shut, and you beat me to the kill, I'd jug you on this slot machine thing. Joey wanted you jugged. Now, what's this between you and slot machines and wheels?"

Sail considered for a while, then took in breath.

"I even went to an institution where they cure things, once," he said. "Kind of a bughouse."

"Huh?"

"One psychologist called it a fixation. I've always had it. Can't help it. Some people can't stand being alone, and some can't stand being shut up in a room, and some can't take mice. With me, it's gambling. Can't stand it. I can't stand the thought of taking chances to make money."

"Just a lad who gets his dough the safe and sane method."

"That's the idea," Sail agreed, "in a general way."

Lester Dent
393 West End Ave
New York City N Y
ENdicott 2-2925

13,000 Words

First Serial Rights

ANGELFISH

By Lester Dent

The spot was a lonely one on a black asphalt sidewalk that
ran among some palm trees and hibiscus bushes.

Lester Dent
393 West End Ave
New York City N Y
ENdicott 2-2925.

13,000 Words

First Serial Rights

ANGELFISH

By Lester Dent

She was a long blue-eyed girl who lay squarely on her back
with the sun shining in her mouth. Her teeth were small and her
tongue was flat, not pointed, and there was about two whiskey
glassfuls of scarlet in her mouth.

When she turned her head slowly on its side, as she did now,
the scarlet emptied out on the black asphalt walk, splashing her
tan columnar neck and the shoulder of her white frock.

Sail kept looking at the gun in his hand. It was a long
black gun. Sail was a long brown man, dressed in black---black
polo shirt, black trousers and black tennis slippers.

The sky overhead was queer, with too much clarity in it. There

Lester Dent,
393 West End Ave.,
New York City, N.Y.
ENdicott 2-2925.

10,000 Words.

ANGELFISH

By Lester Dent

Sterling Drew's life story was inspirational.

To be sure, there was a touch of mystery in it from the first.

One evening, the police arrested a taxi driver for singing on a tenement sidewalk. The crowd which had gathered to listen was blocking the sidewalk, and the city also had an ordinance against street singing.

The taxi driver held his worn cap in his hands and told the magistrate he had been singing to cheer a sick boy. From his bed by one of the tenement windows, the ill boy could hear the singing. The boy had wanted to be a singer. But now he had tb.

An _Evening Star_ reporter investigated. He found the story to be true. The ill boy had passed away with a smile on his wan face, and the taxi driver's song in his heart. At least, that was the way the reporter described it in the human interest feature

which he wrote for the _Evening Star_. The other newspapers got on
the yarn and played it up, for it was nice sob stuff.

Sterling Drew was the taxi driver's name.

A famous radio crooner put Sterling Drew on his national
hookup program as a guest artist. The crooner figured it was a
good publicity stunt. It was. Sterling Drew did one number,
and when he finished, the studio audience was incredibly quiet and
a hardboiled control man took out his handkerchief and blew his
nose and wiped his eyes.

That one song brought in more than thirty thousand letters.
It got Sterling Drew a contract for thirteen weeks at a thousand
dollars a week. He went on three times weekly, but only sang one
song on each program. He insisted on that. It was an excellent
idea, too, because a single song left his listeners with that
strange tight feeling inside, and nothing to relax it.

Sterling Drew became the radio sensation of the year, and also
a puzzle to the writers who did articles for the fan magazines.
For Sterling Drew declined to reveal anything about his past
life. He was a well constructed man physically, tall, angular,
not especially handsome, but with a wistful face which somehow no
one could forget.

Yesterday, I found a face like his, one writer wrote.
I found it in my Bible.

Thousands of fan letters came to this magician of song. He
was said to read all of them---probably he did, because he began
to notice the little notes from Mary Smith. At irregular intervals,
Mary Smith would write, and always only a few lines. Kindly and
sensible words---helpful, too, because they contained small

suggestions that were often excellent. Mary Smith lived in
Miami, Florida.

No details about herself did Mary Smith ever write. When
Sterling Drew went on tour and had an appearance in Miami, he
telephoned Mary Smith that he was sending her two tickets. Over
the telephone, Mary Smith thanked him, ~~but~~ then asked him not to
send the tickets. She was, she explained gently, a helpless
invalid, and because of her heart, her doctor would not permit
her to be taken to the concert. Sterling Drew at once ordered
a taxicab and left his hotel.

As the time arrived for his concert and Sterling Drew
did not appear, those in charge became desperate. They telephoned
everywhere madly. At last, ~~they~~ traced the call which Sterling
Drew had made to Mary Smith, ~~and~~ they got the singer on the
telephone. And when ~~an~~ the announcement was made from the stage
that Sterling Drew was singing to a bedridden invalid, the
audience arose and....

About the time they were cheering, Sterling Drew was looking
into the muzzle of a gun. A ~~~~ ~~slender tanned~~ dark man ~~~~ held the gun
He wore dark ~~blue sandals~~ of unusual design
"We have plans for you," ~~Mary Smith~~ said. "And it's not
what you think!"

~~Sterling Drew stared at the gun, and at the strange slender~~
~~pale figure which held it.~~

~~"Why," he said wonderingly. "You're a man!"~~

Oscar Sail ~~got a telegram~~ had a visitor that same night.
~~He~~ Sail was working on the Diesel motor in his ~~~~
~~eighty eight years old~~ Chesapeake Bay ~~~~

Lester Dent
393 West End Ave
New York N Y
ENdicott 2-2925

13,000 Words

First Serial Rights

ANGELFISH

By Lester Dent

She was a long blue-eyed girl who lay squarely on her back
with the sun shining in her mouth. Her teeth were small and her
tongue was flat, not pointed, and there was about two whiskey
glassfuls of scarlet in her mouth.

When she turned her head slowly on its side, as she did now,
the scarlet emptied out on the black asphalt walk, splashing her
tan columnar neck and the shoulder of her white frock.

Sail stood beside her and kept looking at the gun in his
hand. It was a long black gun. Sail was a long brown man, dressed
in black---black polo shirt, black trousers and black tennis
slippers.

They were very alone, the two of them. The sky overhead was
queer, with too much clarity in it. There was no air stirring.
The palm fronds, the hibiscus leaves all around were as still as
if painted on glass. Seagulls in the air were the only moving
things. And they were not circling. They were flying silently
inland, as if fleeing from something.

Sail ran long fingers slowly through his hair and down hard over the back of his neck. Weather and salt water had not left much color in his hair.

The girl coughed, hackingly.

Sail's mouth looked as if he were holding his tongue with his teeth as he bent to get at her brown leather bag. A chain connected the bag to the girl's wrist. The bag was locked, and Sail opened his pocket knife, punctured the bag and made a slit. His long forefinger raked out loose greenbacks, a flat package and a letter of credit which bore the girl's name. Nan Moberly.

The package was not quite as large as a box of kitchen matches. Sail took it and left the other stuff.

Nan Moberly coughed once more.

"Darn it!" she said. "Some of that red stuff went down the wrong way."

Sail said darkly, "I still think this stunt takes the goofy prize."

"I didn't hire you for your advice. I hired you because you are an honest private detective, if there really is such a thing."

"The advice is thrown in. Nobody in his right mind is going to think you've got a bullet in the lung."

"Put some of that red stuff on the bosom of my dress."

Sail did so. The hole was already in her dress. He pocketed the bottle.

She said, "O.K. I've got a doctor hired to swear I've been shot."

"Take some advice, lady. This---"

"Save it." She coughed again, not as hard. "On with the act."

Her, "Yes," did not move her slightly parted lips.

"I looked at the pictures. That's how I knew. They're pictures put on a film by the cathode ray of a tube in an electrical device which geophysical engineers use to ascertain the contour of rock strata under the earth, as well as whether the strata is porous or dense. The pictures were the record of frequency echo from shots over a certain area. The harder the underground strata, the higher the frequency echo as recorded when picked up on the cathode ray of the tube. If I knew more about it, I could talk on and on."

She said, "You're doing well enough."

Sail said, "At first, I thought it was screwey. But the answer has got to be oil. Geophysical machines locate dome structure favorable to the presence of oil. But they don't guarantee oil is down there. That's where I'm stumped."

"A lake of oil. My company has tapped one end. We don't know which way the lake runs. The pictures show that. They show us where to lease land that will have oil under it."

Sail's, "Mm-m-m," was understanding.

"They're the only pictures that have been shot. It takes weeks of work. Before any other company can work the country, we'll have the land bought or leased. That is---if the wrong people don't get my pictures and make me read them. I'm the only one that can read them, because it was a machine of my design that made them."

"There's no oil around Miami."

"My boss is enroute here from South America. I'm to meet him."
Sail leaned over her. "What's wrong with the setup?"

Lester Dent 20.

Sail straightened up slowly, went to the bed and got one of
the covers which he made into a long hank and placed against the
bathroom door, nudging it snug against the crack with a toe to keep
more of the gas from coming out.

He went back, got the dead man by the hand and dragged him
out from under the bed.

The corpse had gray hair, average height, neat clothing.
There seemed to be nothing wrong with him, except that his neck was
broken.

Sail said, "Who is it? The doctor you hired to help you fake
your story over---Smith---or was that his name?"

Nan Moberly surged up violently on the bed, straining against
the white rope until her arms and legs trembled, then fell back.

She gasped, "Get out of here!"

Sail said, "They weren't fooled by your story. They came here
to get you. The doctor put up a fight and the osteopath fixed his neck.
They made you tell where the pictures were. Now, where are those
men?"

She didn't hesitate. "Your boat. They went to see what
had happened to the osteopath. He went for the pictures and didn't
come back."

"Sure they're not around here? I thought they were in the
bathroom, at first."

"I'm sure," she said levelly.

Sail used his sharp pocket knife on the white ropes which
tied her, then said, "Go to the Floridan and register as---as,
Mary Dallas will do. Stick there until you hear from me or decide
you're not going to. O. K.?"

CAY

By Lester Dent

She was a fair, lean-limbed woman who swam through the dark water in her naked skin. Her hair was long and braided in a pigtail and the end of the pigtail was tied with a string, so the hair did not hamper her swimming.

The night was still, black and warm, and the water was warm. The woman swam in almost complete silence, now that she had managed to stop her sobbing.

The boat was a Chesapeake Bay type of bugeye schooner, thirty-four feet long at the waterline and forty-five overall, with a bottom made of five logs drifted together with Swedish iron rods. The boat had raking masts. Her name was Sail.

Oscar Sail was reading the West Indies Pilot in the bugeye cabin when the scratching came on the hull. The time was nine minutes until eleven, for Sail looked at the clock on his way outside.

"Don't show a light," said the woman in the water.

Sail said, "What in the devil?"

Sail stuck a boathook over the side and felt the woman take

hold of the end. The bugeye sat quiet on the dark water of
the lagoon.

"No," the woman said. "Don't try to pull me aboard."

"Whatever you say," Sail said.

"Are you the tall man?"

"Conceivably."

"I saw you come into the lagoon and drop anchor about
sundown . . . I didn't see anyone else aboard."

After a moment, "I'm alone," Sail said.

"Who are you?"

"Eh?"

"What is your name?"

"David Jones," Oscar Sail said.

His eye pupils had expanded and he could see the prowling
black clouds above, the palm trees on the cay that were like
dark clenched fists held up, and the water that was unnaturally
flat, but the woman was only a pale shape on the end of the
boathook.

"Want to make some money?" she asked.

"Eh?"

"Would you like to make---"

"Why me?"

"Well---you happened to anchor here. There's no other
boat."

"I see."

The woman said, "My boy friend and I want to go to Nassau

Lester Dent,
393 West End Ave.,
New York, N. Y.
ENdicott 2-2925.

10,000 Words.
First North American
Serial Rights.

DEEP

By Lester Dent

Captain Noah caught a shark. He caught it on Sunday. Captain Noah had caught at least five thousand sharks in his lifetime. But this one killed him.

They found Captain Noah sitting in the Gem Theater. The Gem Theater was showing another G-Man picture. "G-Man Guns," the picture was called.

A beef killer is a man with a peculiar occupation. There is no record of a woman beef killer. The beef killer stands at a chute in the stockyards and sticks a thing like an icepick into the base of the beef's brain. Most beef killers use a hammer, though.

A sail needle had been used on Captain Noah. It was some time before they found the needle there.

About the Author

LESTER DENT IN no wise fits the once common conception of the successful writer as a slender, anemic individual as temperamental as a prima donna. Lester packs 218 hard pounds on a six feet, two frame. One time, a group of scribes visited New York Police headquarters and, viewing the training equipment, one bet Lester he couldn't pull his, then, 225 pounds up the forty-feet of climbing rope. Lester won the bet. Off a Missouri farm, for a time handling pipes in the Oklahoma oil fields, Lester has not allowed his muscles to get soft.

Traveler, yachtsman, explorer, aviator in his own right, he has seen much of the world and its people. As a writer, he is one of the most prolific of all.

At earlier time, he has contributed practically the entire contents of a magazine's issue, as is also told of Rupert Hughes in his beginnings.

For the greater part of his work, and with the exception of one period of lapse, Lester has preferred to expend his talents on the greater virility of the rough paper field. However, we believe there are elements and a treatment in the story presented here that point the way to more ambitious accomplishments, which we have an idea will be substantiated when Lester turns seriously to novels.

A great fellow, Lester Dent. Well, they were all great and regular fellows, unaffected by "successful author" phobia on their rapid climb upward.

—Joseph T. Shaw